Murder at Melrose Court

Karen Baugh
MENUHIN

Front cover: Photimageon / Alamy Stock Photo.
Belton House, Grantham, Lincolnshire, England

First paperback and ebook edition December 2018

ISBN: 978-1-7907454-2-5

For Krov
my Darling SK

CHAPTER 1

December 1920

'I must inform you, sir, that a body has been discovered on the front doorstep,' Greggs announced from the doorway.

My concentration was entirely taken up tying a Bibio. Only this morning I'd received a small box of precious seal fur for the precise purpose of creating this seemingly simple fly. The black fluff had required delicate teasing along waxed thread wound around the shaft of the hook, followed by a splash of red. I replaced the long-nosed pliers next to the screwdrivers, grips and whatnot on my workbench, and fumbled for the magnifying glass. All appeared well.

I was vaguely aware of Greggs hovering behind me and creating an annoying distraction – he knew how tricky tying off was.

'I'm busy,' I told him, eyes fixed on the vice holding the lure, scissors poised in one hand, thread held taut in the other.

'Major Lennox, sir,' Greggs persevered. 'It is rather urgent.'

I snipped, then straightened up, the fly complete, and stood back to better survey my work. 'Who is it?'

'I do not know, sir, he is in no condition to furnish a name.'

'What are you talking about, Greggs?' I looked at him sharply, wondering if he'd started early. 'Didn't you ask him?'

'The person on the doorstep is dead, sir,' he replied.

'Dead?'

'Dead, sir.'

Greggs had been my personal batman and butler throughout the four years of the Great War; we both knew more than we wanted to about death, and it seemed to me that he was unlikely to be mistaken in this matter. I left the gunroom briskly and made my way through the hall. Greggs tried to reach the door first – he failed. I yanked it sharply open and walked out into the fresh winter's day. It was crisp and cold with a brisk breeze; sunshine fell upon the body of a large fat man lying on his back across the worn stone flags of my portico.

Greggs was right; the man looked very dead.

'Did you check?' I asked.

'No, sir – back's been playing up.' Greggs motioned vaguely behind him.

'Your paunch is more of an impediment than your spine, Greggs.'

'As you say, sir.'

'Well, best have a look – just in case.' I squatted on my haunches to feel for a pulse – there was nothing. I stood up, and we both looked down.

'I was going fishing in the lake today.'

'Yes, sir.'

'I suppose I'll have to change my plans now.'

'Perhaps so, sir.'

'What do you make of him?'

'Looks a bit shocked, sir.'

Greggs was right: the man's bulging eyes and raised eyebrows had the distinct semblance of surprise about them.

'You'd better call Doctor Fletcher,' I told him as he retreated indoors to the telephone, 'and don't let the operator listen in or the whole village will descend on us.'

I must confess I was somewhat surprised myself – it isn't every day that one encounters death on the door-step. I rubbed my chin and eyed the fellow more closely – who the devil was he? Certainly no one I knew. He was quite distinctive, with a face and figure that would stick in the mind. Bald, with a boxer's nose, cauliflower ears, three or four chins, plump cheeks, froth in the dribble around his gaping mouth – sufficient evidence that the man had breathed his last; but why had he chosen to do it here?

I couldn't see any sign of injury although the body needed to be rolled over to be sure, and I wasn't about to undertake that mammoth task alone.

The door opened; Greggs returned puffing with exertion.

'Sorry for the delay, sir, I notified the doctor and the police,' he said, with some pride in his show of initiative. I couldn't help but smile: Greggs could be an old woman with nitpicking tendencies and over-fond of Irish whiskey, but he was a game old soldier.

'Good man,' I replied. 'Where's Mr Fogg?'

'Probably hiding under your desk, sir.'

'Did he alert you to the body?'

'He did, sir.'

'Always was useless with anything dead.' I glanced at Greggs. It was my observation that all butlers dressed pretty much the same: black tailcoat, white shirt, stiff collar, black dickie and black waistcoat, which showed up crumbs. 'Cook been baking, has she?'

That flustered him, he brushed off specks of biscuit, muttering under his breath.

'Make sure you save some for my tea, and you'd better supply a plate for the Old Bill when they arrive – keep them sweet.'

'Yes, sir. Shall I bring a cushion?

'What the devil for?'

'Put under his head?'

'He's dead, Greggs. What's the point?'

'Show of respect, sir?'

'He may not be in the least bit respectable.'

'Very well, sir,' Greggs sighed, as though I were being unreasonable.

I opened my mouth to protest but he carried on.

'They asked who he was.'

'Who?'

'The police, they wanted to know who was dead,' Greggs said with a hint of expectation. 'You could … examine his garments, sir?'

'Surely they can do that?'

'Yes, sir.'

'Oh, very well.' I bent over the body. His clothes were of the cheap sort: brown coat, greyish shirt, string vest showing between straining buttons, brown suit, brown tie, brown shoes (muddied and scuffed); no hat, nor gloves, no rings nor watch. I flipped through the man's pockets – nothing at all, not even a wallet … except I thought I heard a rustle of paper somewhere inside the coat lining. I felt around and found a hidden slit in the seam and pushed my fingers down to discover a single sheet of folded paper.

I read out the neatly formed copperplate lettering: 'Countess Sophia Androvich Zerevki Polyakov.' I regarded it, frowning. 'Definitely not his name.'

'No, sir.'

'Hmm. You'd better go and call them back – tell them we don't know.'

'Yes, sir.' Greggs went off into the warmth, letting the door slam shut behind him.

It seemed bad form to leave the fellow alone even if he were dead, so not having much else to do I took a walk around him. In doing so, the change of light cast a shadow over his face and revealed a faint indent around his forehead. I looked more closely – he had been wearing a hat not too long ago; the skin showed a faint abrasion where it had rubbed.

I scanned the length of the curving drive up to where the wrought iron gates stood open between high stone walls. No sign of a hat, nor any sign of how its owner had got here. No car parked in the grounds, no motorbike or bicycle, no tyre tracks in the recently raked gravel, the man had simply walked in – I should keep the damn gates shut.

It was possible the hat had fallen off further back, so I strolled up to see if it were lying along the drive. It wasn't, nor was it out in the lane, or under the trees lining the drive, or in the overgrown garden, so I went back to stand under the porch to keep the corpse company.

The police station lay on the other side of the village of Ashton Steeple, just under four miles from The Manor. The Cotswolds country lanes were narrow and winding, so at best they would be another twenty minutes. A sigh of exasperation escaped me as my mind continued to turn over. What was this all about …? And that name – Countess Sophia Androvich Zerevki Polyakov?

My box of cheroots was in a pocket of my tweed jacket; I dug about and pulled one out, lit it with my silver Dunhill and blew smoke into the air as the police arrived with an irritating jangling of alarm bell. The Chief Inspector lowered himself carefully from a highly polished blue Crossley motor car, followed by a sprightly sergeant. The driver, a constable with a round face under a large helmet, remained in the vehicle. He peered out at me, keeping his hand on the rope attached to the brass bell on the car's roof – presumably in the hope of ringing it again.

'Good day to you, Major Lennox,' Chief Inspector Rawlins said, tugging his coat over his crumpled suit to button up against the cold.

'Inspector Rawlins.' I nodded politely in greeting. I was surprised to see he was still in service – the last I'd seen of him was before the War, and he was verging on the decrepit then.

We wasted no more time in pleasantries. His rheumy eyes turned from me to the fat man forming a mound at my feet. He and the sergeant stood in silent observation for a moment, closely watched by the bobby in the car.

'Take a look at him, Walker,' the Inspector ordered.

Sergeant Walker snapped into action; he removed his helmet by lifting the strap to tip it forward, and placed it carefully on the stone flags, then tugged up his uniform trousers to preserve the sharply pressed creases, and knelt by the body to examine the neck, chest, face, hands and wrists of the deceased.

'Dead, sir,' Walker declared, turning towards his boss, long face frowning in earnest. 'An' I can't see nothin' that killed 'im. No blood nor nowt.'

'Any identity on him?' the Inspector asked, watching the sergeant closely.

Walker rummaged around in the clothing, turning pockets inside out, and even looking under the tie.

'No. Not on 'is person, but we might find somethin' if we turn 'im over.'

'Easier said than done, my boy, but I'm sure you'll manage.' The Inspector straightened up, coughed with a loud wheeze of the chest, then turned to me. 'He was visiting you, then?'

'No, he was not,' I stated quite clearly to remove any doubt about the matter.

'So what was he doing here?' the Inspector demanded.

'I have no idea.'

He stared up at me from under beetle brows; which was irritating, so I stared back.

'I think someone killed him, Major Lennox.'

'Don't be ridiculous, Inspector. He's had a heart attack by the looks of him. You must have seen enough examples.'

'Ah, but you may be tryin' to devise a subterfuge.' Rawlins stepped forward and looked me straight in the eye from a very short distance.

'Damn poor subterfuge to leave him on my own doorstep,' I snapped back.

'Did you kill 'im?'

'No, I did not. Nobody did. He keeled over of his own accord, just look at him!'

Rawlins and Walker both duly turned to stare at the body, which was looking more blue around the gills as time ticked by. I think even they realised that no murder had been done.

Inspector Rawlins took a deep breath, coughed, and tried a different tack. 'You livin' 'ere now, Major Lennox?'

'Yes, of course. Where do you think I'm living?'

'Thought you might of gone off to London after your father died. This 'ouse is big for just one man, and it needs a fair bit of work doin', don't it?'

I looked up at my family home, an old, mellow-bricked Queen Anne house; dusty, draughty, cluttered, and with an air of genteel decay about it.

'What does the state of my house have to do with finding a body on the doorstep?'

''E might of fallen off the roof, or a ladder. Maybe 'e was fixin' something for you, an' it was dangerous, an' you don't want to admit it.' He leaned forward and wagged a finger under my nose. 'That's negligence, that is!'

'Considering the size of the man, he was hardly likely to be up a ladder.'

'Everyone knows you like shootin' things, Major Lennox.' Sergeant Walker had picked up his helmet and was holding it under his arm and joined in the interrogation.

'It is patently obvious that he was not shot,' I pointed out. 'And I shoot pheasant and game, not people.'

'If 'e was tryin' 'is hand at burglerin', you might 'ave tried to scare 'im off,' Walker added.

'Good thinking, lad,' Rawlins added in support, 'and he could have been trying to break in up a ladder.'

'Greggs!' I jerked open the front door and started shouting for Greggs to come and tell them how he'd found the body, when we were interrupted by a red Riley Eleven driven at speed through the gateway. It drew up in a spray of gravel and Doctor Cyril Fletcher jumped out, nattily dressed as usual in tweeds and plus fours, sporting a trim moustache and carrying a leather medical case. He raised his hat to the policemen, then came to shake my hand, grinning with affection.

'Well, well, Lennox. A body! Pheasant is more your style, isn't it? – what have you been doing?' Cyril Fletcher joshed.

'I did not shoot him, Cyril. Will you please inform the constabulary that this man has not been shot.'

'Ha! They giving you a hard time, old chap?' He turned to the Inspector. 'No blood, Rawlins, he can't have been shot.'

'He must have fallen,' Rawlins retorted.

'No, there would still be blood, from his nose or ears most likely,' the Doctor told him as he stooped to examine the whale-like corpse. He stood up. 'Need to roll him over.'

We looked at each other; the Inspector coughed meaningfully.

'Oh, very well,' I conceded, and bent to put my arms under the fat man's shoulders. 'Get the torso, Sergeant. Cyril, turn the legs.'

We heaved, pushing hard, rocking him to gain momentum, and finally rolled him onto his stomach with a thud as he slumped face down onto the stone flags; then we stood back breathing heavily. No blood, no knife, no nasty wound – nothing to see other than the creases in the damp coat and some snags in the trousers.

'Not a thing,' I said.

'Ay, don't look like much.' Sergeant Walker straightened up, looking disappointed about the absence of evidence of dramatic death.

'Best check him over, my lad, just to be sure,' the Inspector ordered.

'Yes, sir,' Walker replied with a note of despondency. A grey cloud slid across the sun as the sergeant examined the body and again failed to find anything significant.

Greggs emerged with a tray of tea and biscuits, which managed to entice the bobby out of the vehicle, although he was shooed back in again by Inspector Rawlins.

'He's looking after the car. It's new,' he imparted. 'We're modernising the police force. Very important work we have now, making sure those Germans don't come back.' He looked slowly around the property as if to check that we hadn't been invaded recently.

Cyril Fletcher raised his eyebrows as we exchanged glances.

'Take him to the mortuary, Inspector, I'll have a better look at him there,' Fletcher ordered. 'Heart attack looks the most likely culprit, so I doubt there's anything here for you gentleman to concern yourselves with.'

The Doctor replaced his cup and saucer on the tray and turned to follow me into the house as Greggs held the door open.

'Apart from the lack of any identification,' Chief Inspector Rawlins intoned.

We turned around to regard the policeman.

'There was that paper, sir,' Greggs reminded me in his helpful fashion.

'Ah yes – one moment.' I dug out the folded sheet of paper from my inside pocket and handed it over. 'I found this.'

'This could be an important clue! You should have given this to me when I arrived, Major Lennox.' The Chief Inspector wagged his finger at me in an annoying fashion.

'My apologies, Inspector, I forgot about it.'

'I hope you're not hiding anything, sir. It does seem strange that this man has died on your doorstep and you not knowing him. Or so you say.'

'I can assure you, Inspector, I have no idea whatsoever who this man is,' I replied with feeling.

The Inspector read out the name on the paper, stumbling over the foreign words. 'Countess Sophia Androvich Zerevki Polyakov ...' He stared up at me. 'And you don't know who she is either?'

'No, I do not.' Except that I did, and the day suddenly seemed a lot more complicated than when it had started.

CHAPTER 2

Mr Fogg was indeed under my desk in the library. I enticed him out with a dog biscuit from the top drawer.

'Silly mutt.' I stroked his head affectionately. Fogg by name, fog by nature. He was a golden cocker spaniel of very little brain, and hated dead bodies of any description. He gazed back with liquid brown eyes, wagging his stump of a tail and his backside in excitement as I passed him another treat. The police had gone, the Manor and grounds were peaceful again and our little household was much the happier for it.

Mr Fogg had been Father's gift to me just before he died. The day the armistice was signed, I walked into our Royal Flying Corps quarters in France, ordered Greggs to pack and follow, and then flew back to this house in my old Sopwith Camel. Pa was pretty much on his last legs; Ma had died years earlier, so there had been no loving wife to care for him. I did my best, but the old man expired before spring arrived in 1919. Fogg had been handed over at our last Christmas together, a runtish puppy with a sweet nature, and had ever since been my constant companion.

A sigh escaped me as I glanced at the pile of papers on my desk – mostly unpaid bills. I swept them aside, reached for the decanter and poured myself a shot of whisky. No fishing today nor tomorrow because it was set to snow.

I stared absently at my books, ranged randomly along shelves built long ago. Besides the gunroom, the library was my favourite: cluttered, cosy and filled with mismatched furniture according to the taste of Lennox men down the generations. Damn it, what was that corpse all about? And the name of the Russian countess on the hidden paper?

A knock on the door interrupted my reverie. I drained my glass, reached over to switch on my desk lamp, and shouted, 'Enter.'

'Telegram, sir!' Tommy Jenkins brought it in – he was the house boot boy and was Cook's nephew. He was deputising for Greggs, who had gone to lie down with a dram or two, with which I sympathised; I wouldn't have minded doing the same.

'Read it out.'

'Yes, sir.' Tommy Jenkins pulled off his cap, shoved it into his pocket and swept his hair out of his eyes. 'Sorry I missed out this morning, sir. ''Ad to be in the village pickin' up groceries, sir. Aunty said that man was 'uge. She went to 'ave a look while they was liftin' 'im into the wagon.'

It had been a taxing afternoon. More bobbies had assembled and the Inspector had officiated as they tried to heave the body into an ambulance on a stretcher that didn't so much stretch as bend almost to breaking point. I had opted to watch the proceedings while Greggs made more tea and Cook provided biscuits for the assorted crew. Once the fat man was loaded into the van, the police searched the grounds and gardens while the Inspector insisted we each sign statements. A few locals turned up having heard the news, and offered advice as they thought fit; naturally Greggs and Cook had to cater for them too. By the time they all drove off, the place had taken on the atmosphere of a village fete.

'Just read the telegram, Jenkins.'

'Ay, sir.' His round-eyed face glowed with excitement; no one had ever died with such drama in the neighbourhood. 'An' nobody knows who 'e was neither. But the grocer said 'e saw a strange motor go down the 'igh street an' turn up the lane toward 'ere, sir. Then ten minutes later it came back again!'

'What sort of car was it?'

'Don't know, sir.'

'Go and find out.'

'Yes, sir.' The boy turned to dash off.

'Wait! Read the telegram first.'

'Ay, sir.' He came back to stand in front of my desk and lifted the telegram to read slowly, one word at a time. 'Lord Melrose kindly invites you to Melrose Court for the forthcoming festivities. Stop. Please come. Stop. Important news to impart. Stop. Your Loving Uncle. Stop.'

He placed the grubby square of yellow card bearing an official red Post Office stamp on my desk and left at a run. I tossed it onto the pile of papers and sighed. The formal invitation from Melrose Court was in there somewhere; I hadn't yet replied because I didn't want to go – but didn't want to upset Uncle either. Given today's events, maybe I'd better accept? I ran a hand through my hair and looked at the pile of paper again. If my shares don't buck up, I'll have to sell something soon to settle that lot.

My hand reached for the whisky decanter, but I held off; too easy to take that route.

Flakes of snow were swirling in the grey sky. I went over to stoke the fire and then settled beside the hearth in my favourite chair. Rubbing my jaw, I thought back over the day's events.

The Countess Sophia Androvich Zerevki Polyakov – she was a White Russian, one of the Tsarists who had escaped when the Bolshevik Revolution overran the country in 1917. Having lost their homes, their lands and their peasants, the Russian aristocrats were selling gold and jewellery to survive. But Countess Sophia wasn't, she was buying, and I knew she had a knowledgeable and expensive eye.

I was frowning into the flames with Fogg at my feet and a tray of coffee at my elbow when Tommy rapped on the library door. He came in holding his cap and fidgeting with excitement.

'Car was an Austin Seven, sir, dark blue, bit battered. Mr Benson the grocer didn't know nothin' more, but 'e reckoned it were from London, sir.'

'Why did he think it was from London?'

'Cos it weren't from round 'ere.'

'Did anyone else notice anything about it?'

'My mate Billy saw it drive past the post office; 'e said there were two men in it, both wearin' 'ats pulled low so 'e couldn't see nothin' clear on their faces.'

'Is the post office coming into the village or going out of it?'

Tommy blinked. 'Don't you know where the post office is?'

'No, why should I?'

This seemed to confound the lad. 'But everyone knows that.'

'Well, I don't.'

He looked at me as though I were an idiot. 'It depends where you're startin' from, sir.'

'London, of course.'

'You think they were from London too?'

'No, I've no idea where they were from. You said they went past the post office and the grocer thought they came from London.'

'Ah, but we don't know for sure they was comin' from London, do we, sir? Can't be makin' assumptions, my Aunty always says: "If you just assume summat it's no better'n guessin."'

I really did need that drink.

'Tommy, in or out?'

'Comin' in o' course. You ain't very observant, sir. You need to be lookin' about a bit more.'

'Yes, thank you, Tommy. Did Billy or the grocer see anything useful – like a number plate?'

'No, sir, an' nor did no one else. I asked as many as I could, which is most people that matters.'

I doubted that but tossed Tommy a sixpence anyway; he headed off toward the kitchen with a grin on his face.

It was no surprise, I reflected, that the grocer thought the car was from London: anything that wasn't local was instantly assumed to come from the city, and in that regard the assumption was probably correct. Where was the hat? The fat man had worn a hat. The police had searched the grounds and lanes round about but had failed to find anything of note. The man's money and papers would almost certainly be in a fold inside the hat – it was the habit among poorer people living in big cities where pickpockets were rife. Hat snatchers too – although anyone as big and tall as the dead man would likely have been beyond the reach of most thieves. And besides, this is rural England, we don't have robbers lurking in the hedgerows. No, the man's hat was taken by the person who drove him here in the Austin Seven. But why was it more important to take the hat than to help the dying man? I continued staring into the fire until dinner was announced.

Next morning I had Greggs pack my carpet bag, and Tommy was loading it into the back of my brand new black Bentley 3-Litre when the telephone in the hall rang.

'Doctor Fletcher is awaiting you on the apparatus, sir,' Greggs announced as he came out onto the flagstones in front of the porch, now mercifully free of corpses but covered with a thin layer of snow. I was under the bonnet, checking the engine, which was ticking over with a distinct hiccup. I returned to the hall.

'Lennox,' Fletcher's voice boomed from the receiver. 'Can you hear me?'

I held the contraption away from my ear and bellowed into the transmitter cup on the candlestick stand. 'Yes, loud and clear, over.'

'He had a heart attack.'

'The fat man?'

'Yes, of course, the fat man. How many corpses did you find yesterday!'

'Very amusing, Cyril – what are the police doing? Over.'

There was a distinct rattle and intake of breath heard by both of us.

'Milly, get off the line,' Cyril Fletcher shouted at the operator, who was apt to listen in on calls rather than just switching them through as she was supposed to.

I heard the clunk as she cut herself off.

'Cyril. Are you still there?' I shouted.

'Certainly I am. The police have little to say in the matter now, but I need to send some samples away for analysis. I'm certain he died of natural causes, unless you poisoned him, haha.'

'No, he was dead when I met him. Thank you for calling, Cyril, I'm pleased to hear the diagnosis – the last thing I need is the police around my neck, over.'

'You don't have to keep saying "over", Lennox.'

'Very well. Over.'

'I'll inform you when I have more news. Have a nice Christmas!' Fletcher bellowed.

'And to you too … Over.'

I handed the device back to Greggs and noticed both the maids hanging over the upstairs banister rail. They ran off giggling when I frowned up at them.

Well, that was one less botheration. I returned to the Bentley to find Fogg already in the passenger seat, the engine purring and my favourite fishing rod strapped to the side. I jumped in and we set off for Melrose Court in the deeper vales of the Cotswolds. An open-top tourer may seem an eccentric option given the drifting snow, but it was a machine of power and beauty and the next best thing to flying. I wore my old Royal Flying Corps helmet, goggles, silk scarf, leather trench coat and driving gloves. It was freezing cold, but it gave me the chance to open up the engine and give the car a really good blast.

An hour later, Fogg and I pulled up outside the gatehouse at Melrose Court and waited for the lodge-keeper to open up. The house stood at the end of a long drive lined with snow-laden trees. I pulled the throttle and roared down it making a tremendous noise before coming to a halt at the steps of the portico in front of the old Georgian mansion. Uncle's redoubtable butler, Cooper, opened the outsize front door to walk out onto the broad top step just as I climbed from the car.

'Cooper! How goes the household?' I threw the keys to him as I entered, stripped off my driving coat, goggles and external paraphernalia to load onto a footman, and dropped the carpet bag on the chequered floor tiles as Fogg dashed on ahead.

Cooper was opening his mouth to respond when Uncle called to me from the bottom of the stairs, waving his walking stick. 'Heathcliff! My dear boy, how delightful to see you.'

I went over and gave him an affectionate hug and a grin.

'Likewise, Uncle, and don't call me Heathcliff.'

Dear Uncle Charles. He seemed to be shrinking with age. His hair had grown white and wispy above his benign phiz, and he looked more like an old monk with a fondness for brandy with every passing year.

'Oh, very well – Lennox, then! Don't know why you took such a dislike to Heathcliff, your lovely mother was very proud of it, you know. She was a romantic soul, such a dreamer. We all loved her.'

'Yes, Uncle, and we miss her, too. Damned embarrassing name though, she could have used it for a dog if she were that keen.' I glanced at my dog, who had been rushing around our heels but was now heading upstairs toward the drawing room, where he knew tea and cake were frequently to be found.

'Now, now, my boy. I'm so very pleased you are here with us. What do you think of the decorations – aren't they splendid?' Uncle Charles waved his stick toward the lofty walls of the hall, hung with wreaths of glossy green holly and bunches of bright red berries interspersed with swags of ivy woven with golden ribbons. I'd already negotiated the huge Christmas tree and we turned to admire the array of candles, painted wooden figures and winged angels. As always, the tree was placed opposite the roaring log fire and filled the place with the scent of pine. I felt a tug of emotion; it stirred memories of our traditional family Christmases when we were more numerous.

'Wonderful, very festive.' I sought to change the subject. 'So you finally installed a telephone line.'

'I did, yes indeed. How did you guess?' Uncle raised bushy white eyebrows in surprise.

'Because you've come down to greet me. If the lodge-keeper hadn't been able to telephone through to the house, you wouldn't have known I was here until Cooper informed you.'

'Haha! You always were a clever boy, your father thought so too. Poor Hugh, I do miss him.' He stopped to peer up at me. 'Do you know they have machines that make music nowadays? It's quite dreadful.'

'Yes, of course I do. Come upstairs, Uncle.' I took his arm to lead him on. Despite the enormous fireplace blazing with logs, it was still draughty in the hall, and I didn't want the old man to catch a chill.

It was slow going and Uncle was tottering more than usual.

'Have you heard my news, Heathcliff? It is of great importance. I wanted to tell you myself.'

'No, and stop calling me Heathcliff.'

'Very well, very well, my dear boy. But I am aflame with excitement.'

'Really?' That did make me raise my brows. 'You'd better spit it out then.'

'I'm engaged!' Uncle stopped on the stairs, eyes alight with excitement. 'I have a fiancée. Isn't it marvellous?'

I looked at him, seeing him suddenly boyish with enthusiasm. 'I'm delighted to hear it. Astonished, but delighted. Do I know the lady?'

'I doubt it, she's fresh from France, we met quite recently, but I fell head over heels. At my age, too! I never imagined anyone would be able to replace my dear Mary, but there you have it. I've lost my heart like an old fool.'

'Congratulations, Uncle. Someone to care for you is exactly what you need.' I was still trying to encourage him up the staircase, but we weren't making much progress.

'She's waiting for us in the drawing room. She has been here for over a week already, her niece too – for propriety's sake, you know. But we've had a marvellous time. They are staying over for Christmas and then we shall be wed. I am the most fortunate of men, Heathcliff.'

'Excellent, Uncle.' I managed to steer him into the first-floor corridor. 'Who did you say she was?'

He stopped again and turned to me, his face beaming. 'Countess Sophia Androvich Zerevki Polyakov,' he jubilantly replied.

CHAPTER 3

That caught me on the blindside, but I managed to stutter a few light remarks without attracting questions as we reached the drawing-room doors. I readied myself for the encounter, arranging my expression into a sort of frozen amiability. Now was the moment – would the Countess know who I was?

Cooper, good butler that he was, had rushed up the back stairs and was waiting with gloved hand on handle as we arrived; then with practised ease he swung open the door and we entered unannounced.

No ladies were present in the room. I retained a sigh of relief while Uncle's face fell as realisation dawned that his dear Sophia was no longer present. He looked around, mouth slightly agape. 'Where is she?' he stuttered at the drawing room's only inhabitant.

Sir Peregrine Kingsley rose from the largest sofa, put aside the financial newspaper he'd been reading, and came over to greet us.

'Ah, dear Charles – and you too, Heathcliff, what a pleasure to see you again, old chap.'

I nodded stiffly to him. Peregrine bloody Kingsley was lawyer and adviser to Uncle and one of the reasons I had been reluctant to accept the Christmas invitation; he was a distant relation of sorts, too smug by half and the cause of many a family tiff over the years.

'But where is Sophia?' Uncle asked again.

A smile played across Peregrine Kingsley's lips. 'There was a commotion,' he explained loftily. 'A dog came in with a footman, jumped up and caused the Countess to spill tea over her dress. The ladies became rather agitated; I tried to help of course, but they felt the need to retreat to the Countess's rooms to remedy the situation,' Kingsley expounded, wafting his arm about, a trail of eau de cologne flowing in its wake. 'The dress, you know. Silk. Quite ruined.'

'Fogg,' I remarked curtly. 'He didn't mean any harm. They'll have to get used to him.'

'Yes, yes, but I think I should go and see that they are settled,' Uncle Charles fretted, and grew agitated, and began waving his stick about. 'Ladies can be highly strung, you know, and they are foreigners in a foreign land. Cooper, be a good fellow and escort me, would you.'

The old man tottered off, leaning heavily on Cooper's arm. That left Sir Peregrine bloody Kingsley and me in the room, which incidentally had been spruced up. There were new cushions with flowery covers on the sofas, which I saw had been recently upholstered in pale-yellow satin-type stuff; and the walls had been painted to match. Even the ornate plasterwork had been given a new coat of paint, though the old carved marble fireplace had survived sans embellishment. I dislike change, and it made me more antipathetic than usual toward the lawyer, who now turned his smug phiz toward me.

'Surprised to see you here, Heathcliff,' he pronounced. 'I understood your presence wasn't expected. Rather fortuitous, though – we have business to discuss.'

I eyed him coolly – he had an Alpine tan, swept-back silver hair, and was dressed like a bloody mannequin.

'It's Christmas, I haven't come here to talk numbers with you. And don't call me Heathcliff.'

'As you wish,' Kingsley replied smoothly. 'But it isn't numbers, old man, it's your Uncle's will. He's asked me to rewrite it; it concerns yourself, and cousin Edgar, of course. I'd like to explain the implications to you both.'

'Then Uncle can tell Edgar and me about it himself. After your monumental incompetence, there's nothing on earth I wish to discuss with you. Take my advice and don't try to push yourself beyond your limited bounds, Kingsley.'

I turned around and stalked out, going upstairs to my rooms in the east wing, where I found Cooper hovering in the corridor, fingering his collar. He was probably much the same age as Uncle and also white of hair, but very upright, sprightly of step, and although dressed in much the same rig as Greggs, the get-up was vastly more streamlined.

'Hurrumph, sir.' Cooper coughed unconvincingly as I reached for the door handle.

I frowned. 'What?'

'We have reallocated you, sir.'

'What?'

'Your rooms have been reallocated, sir, and your personal items have been removed to another part of the house, sir. The Italian suite in the west wing, overlooking the front.'

I stalled in my tracks, shoved my hands in pockets and stared in surprise and irritation at him.

'These have been my rooms in this house since I was just out of short trousers, Cooper. All my old stuff's in there and has been for years. What the devil is the meaning of this?'

'Her Ladyship. Urhum. The Countess, that is, sir. She rather took a fancy to these rooms, and she requested the use of them, so His Lordship had your belongings moved to the Italian suite. I'm sure he meant to inform you, sir.'

The butler had turned red but maintained a stoic dignity as I gave him my best steely-eyed glare. That didn't achieve much, so I turned on my heel and took off for the west wing, Cooper valiantly trying to keep up with me.

The Italian suite was ornamented with gilded putti, Venetian mirrors and trompe l'oeil from floor to ceiling – exactly the sort of place you'd expect to find a French dancing-master mincing about, or a pricy tart in her knickers.

'No –' I looked it up and down '– it's got angels on the ceiling! Out of the question. Looks like a bloody bordello, Cooper.'

'I'm afraid I'm not familiar with such establishments, sir.'

'Er, no, well, neither am I – but I imagine it does … not that I imagine such things. Never mind, Cooper.' This was getting tricky, I switched track. 'Why the devil didn't you put the Countess in here?'

'She requested rooms closer to His Lordship, sir.'

That took the wind out of my sails; couldn't argue against womanly sentiment. 'Right.' I ran fingers through my hair. 'Well, move everything to the Blue rooms at the back, and don't argue with me, Cooper.'

'No, sir. Certainly sir.'

Disconcerted and feeling a trifle low, I called for my dog and coat and stomped off for a long walk through the snow-strewn woods.

'Blanket,' I demanded of the footman when he opened the front door to us.

I'd given orders for a dog blanket to be made available to rub down Mr Fogg on our return, and the footman had kept it to hand for that very purpose. Fogg was duly rubbed, bundled up and taken to the kitchens for a meal, a cuddle by the kitchen maids and a warm lodging by the stove until all the mud fell off.

I went up to survey my new lodgings in the north-west corner; the Blue rooms had been decorated through the decades in various shades of the colour, many of which could be seen exposed in layers peeling from the wood-work. The wallpaper of dainty forget-me-nots had faded sufficiently to be inoffensive, and the smell of damp, mouse droppings and woodsmoke was so familiar that it was barely worth noting. The rooms were inconvenient and over-furnished with outdated pieces from the rest of the house, including a four-poster bed, a couple of oak coffers, and some antique carved cupboards set against the walls. Upon opening one, I discovered my jerseys carefully stacked and folded in waxed paper and strewn with mothballs.

My books had been placed in an age-blackened book-shelf, and I picked through them to choose a few to pile on my bedside table, with Moby Dick on top, it being my favourite. Then I threw some more coal on the fire and gave it a good jab with the poker to keep it blazing because, quite frankly, it was bloody freezing in there.

I hadn't been in these rooms since Edgar and I were children playing hide and seek, so I was unsure where anything was. Behind what appeared to be a cupboard door I found an unheated bathroom with mahogany and brass fittings, and next to it a large dressing room with a spacious built-in closet, fitted with numerous shelves and racks. This had been filled with my hunting garb, hats, caps, boots, shoes, fishing gear and my collection of guns – the guns I kept here, that was, not the ones I had at home. I looked up and around, switched on and off the lights – which didn't work – and then went to test the wing chair set before the fireplace. The rooms were to my liking; comfortable, old-fashioned, and reminiscent of my own home at the Manor.

There was still enough daylight to see quite well

outside, so I crossed to the windows. The bedroom overlooked the stable block and outhouses; servants were dashing across the snowy courtyard between the house and outbuildings. Marvellous! Very interesting to watch them at work; I'd never been sure what they did when the family wasn't around, and now I had an excellent opportunity to observe. I sat in the window seat and remained there until it grew dark. Then I drew the curtains, lit an oil lamp and a couple of candles and dressed for dinner while contemplating the inevitable meeting with Countess Sophia, my new Aunt-to-be.

Making my way briskly downstairs in the direction of the drawing room, I was diverted by the thought of Cuban cigars, so I swung into the smoking room to take my pick from the humidor. Someone was already in there: I heard Peregrine bloody Kingsley clearing his throat. Fortunately, the room was dimly lit and I hadn't been spotted, so I started to back out. But I paused when I heard a female voice.

'Peregrine, please be careful. I do not wish to cause upsets.'

'Oh Natasha, my dear,' Peregrine Kingsley replied. 'Just seeing you, being close to you, it is enough and yet…'

'Do not say more. There is much we need to think of.'

'Please don't worry. I am your faithful and loving servant, my darling girl. I will do anything for you, Anything.'

I exited quietly, eyebrows raised. Natasha must be the Countess's niece. I knew Kingsley to be a ladies' man, but surely he was old enough to be her father!

Christmas was beginning to look peculiarly singular this year.

Cousin Edgar was the only inhabitant of the drawing room, and I was mightily pleased to see him.

Edgar was my double cousin and younger than me by a month – we had been brought up almost as brothers and had always felt as though we were. The family background is convoluted: Uncle Charles, being the oldest, had inherited the estate and the title of eighth Lord Melrose. His younger brother and sister, Hugh and Caroline, had married two American siblings, Mary-Rose and Bertrand Coleman, both wealthy heirs to the same oil fortune. All this made for a close and surprisingly happy family. Each of the younger couples had a son: Hugh had sired me, and Caroline had given birth to Edgar Coleman. Uncle Charles, who'd married Mary, failed to produce any living children; consequently the title would one day fall on me, and so would the estate and funds – or at least that had been the intention until now.

'Edgar! You're here, thank God! Between lawyers and foreigners, I was beginning to feel like a stranger in the house.'

'Lennox, how the devil are you? I thought you were going to bail. I just arrived a half hour ago, it's snowing a blizzard – had a terrible trip down on the train, stopped at every damn station between Paddington and Melrose,' Edgar laughed, shaking my hand and warmly embracing me. 'Uncle is resting, and Cooper warned me Peregrin Kingsley's here, soon to be followed by son Adam and his wife. Thought we were going to be outnumbered by the Kingsley clan! Can't tell you how pleased I am to see you, old man.'

I laughed with him; it was a terrific treat to see him again. 'Why can't they find other relatives to sponge off?' I complained. 'They turn up every damn Christmas like a recurring plague.'

'Ha, they won't find such an easy touch as Uncle anywhere else. Except you, maybe.' He eyed me as he spoke, but I chose to ignore the jibe.

Grinning, he sat back down and picked up a goblet of brandy from the table next to his elbow. 'To you, Lennox, and another Melrose Christmas.'

'Hang on. Let me get a glass, I'm in need of a snifter, too.'

Rather than pull the bell for Cooper, I poured it myself from the decanter on the sideboard and dropped into a fireside chair opposite him. I must say Edgar was looking very natty with his dark hair slicked back in the new style, with a dab of oil to keep it in place. I raised my glass and we took a warming sip of excellent brandy.

'You're looking remarkably well, Edgar. New tailor?'

He brushed a hand over the lapel of the extremely well-cut suit he was sporting. 'Yes, Savile Row! Hellish pricey, but worth every penny I'd say. Requirement of the job to look the part, you know!'

'No, I don't know and never have. The diplomatic corps or whatever you call it is a world away from my rural retreat, and that's the way I like it.'

'Told you many a time, Lennox, you need to get out and about in the world, you're rusticating away in the middle of nowhere. Completely wasted, old man.' He leaned back in his chair, his long legs crossed. 'Our foreign skulduggery may not interest you, but there's plenty of home-grown intrigue that could use your abstract intellect.'

'Abstract intellect! What the devil is that supposed to mean?'

'Erratic. Your brain bounces around, always has, then comes out with something completely unexpected in the end.' Edgar always did have a way of sugaring his insults.

'I'll take my erratic brain elsewhere if you keep talking such drivel,' I retorted, and then switched to the subject uppermost in my mind. 'I assume you know about the engagement?'

'Yes, of course I know – I introduced them. Countess Sophia is a delightful lady, full of fun.' He regarded me closely over his glass, observing my reaction, which I hid as best I could.

'Well, I'm relieved to hear that – although you could have mentioned it.'

Edgar drew out two slim French cigars and tossed one to me, lighting his own with a heavy gold lighter, and blew smoke toward the ceiling. I followed suit, savouring the taste.

'Been on my travels; and anyway you're a worst correspondent than I am,' he said in his defence.

Which was true, although I wasn't going to admit it.

Edgar turned a tad more serious. 'I'm sorry, Lennox, I was going to write but it was pretty quick and all a bit complicated. I'm relieved you're here so I can tell you face to face.'

'As you damn well should. Uncle dropped the news on me today. It sounded like a whirlwind romance straight out of some ghastly penny dreadful.'

'Ha, well, it wasn't that bad.' Edgar laughed quietly. 'Poor Uncle, touched at last by the old urges.'

'Touched, anyway,' I replied wryly. 'So where did you encounter the Countess?'

'Paris.' Edgar answered through a cloud of smoke. 'I was staying at the embassy for a few days and met Sophia at one of the balls. She's one of the White Russian emigrés – escaped the Bolshevik revolution back in '17. There's a whole enclave of them in Paris now.'

'Yes, I know.'

'Really? You know her?'

'I mean I know about them being in Paris; how they escaped Russia after all the battles and bombings and such. I've heard about it – I mean, read about it in the papers, you know.' I was babbling, a bad habit when nervous, so I swiftly changed tack. 'How did you introduce her to Uncle Charles? He never leaves the country.'

'She'd come over to London, not sure why. Probably selling jewels or some such – most of the Russian gentry grabbed their portables and fled when the Reds took over. They've been providing a nice supply of fancy baubles ever since. Anyway, I was invited to the ex-Russian Ambassador's London house for a soirée, and she was there. She had her niece Natasha with her on that occasion – rather an attractive girl actually. We bumped into each other from time to time, and when Uncle came to visit his Harley Street quack he stayed at my flat, and I asked Sophia and Natasha to dine with us. Which all went rather well.'

'Judging by their engagement, it must have gone extremely well!'

Edgar laughed. 'Haven't seen the old man so happy in a very long while – he's quite dotty about the whole thing. Personally, I think it'll do him a world of good: she'll chivvy him up, get him going again, don't you think?'

I nodded slowly. 'Yes, I imagine so. But … how much do you really know about her, Edgar? It's all a bit sudden. Is she who she says she is?'

'Oh, come now, Lennox, I met her in the best possible circles; she wouldn't be able to cross the doorstep of those rarified enclaves if she weren't top notch.' He jabbed his cigar in my direction. 'And although you may not think so, I am an excellent judge of character. Part of my job, you know – can't make a mistake in my line, too damned dangerous.'

It crossed my mind to tell him some of my experiences, but for the moment I decided to hold off until I'd met the lady herself. It was quite possible the encounter would bring the whole story to light pretty quickly anyway.

Edgar tossed the remains of his cigar into the fire. 'You do realise that Peregrine Kingsley is here because of the will, don't you?'

'Yes, he told me. Couldn't wait to tell me, actually. Bloody parasite. Given his useless financial advice, I'd be very surprised if there was anything left worth inheriting.'

'Oh God, you didn't act on anything he recommended, did you?'

My shoulders dropped: the whole subject left me despondent. 'Yes, to my lasting shame. He swore to me that Eastern Railroad stock was not only a sure bet, but it was going to triple within the year.' I got up and fetched the decanter from the sideboard and topped up our glasses.

'Didn't they go bankrupt?'

'They did, and took a significant amount of my money down with them.' I swilled my drink around in the glass, then downed it in one.

Edgar frowned. 'Lennox how could you be so stupid? You know what Kingsley is, you've known how unreliable he is for years.'

'Yes, of course I know. But he was just so convincing; he sent me the newspapers and the stock reports. And I wasn't the only one, lots of people bought into it – hundreds, probably.'

'But you loathe Kingsley, why on earth did you even talk to him?'

'House is mortgaged, and my funds won't cover the interest. I was being dunned quite nastily. I wrote and asked him for the name of anyone who could provide re-financing, and he put me on to the stock scheme.'

'You should have asked me first!'

'Couldn't find you. You'd disappeared off on one of your trips somewhere.' I let an exasperated sigh escape my lips. 'I've never had your knack with money, Edgar. It doesn't interest me; my eyes glaze over just thinking about it.'

'No excuse, Lennox. Your side of the family were always useless with money. All grew up rich, not one of you understood a damn thing about pounds, shillings and pence. If they'd had any sense, they'd have made sure you were educated in estate management rather than waste your time sporting and hunting.'

'Nobody had any sense Edgar, only your father. Ma wasn't expected to worry about money; I doubt she even knew what it was, and Pa's side were just as bad.'

'Pops taught me finance because his family had built up the oil business, they'd had to work for it, money didn't just fall around their ears. When they sold the company, he made sure I'd be self-reliant by tying up all of my inheritance until I produce legitimate offspring,' Edgar laughed. 'Totally bonkers but it's never done me any harm. It's rather satisfying to earn my own crust, actually.' He looked at me, concern creasing his brow. 'Is it so bad?'

I poured myself another snifter and slumped back in my chair. 'After Ma died, Pa tried to handle the funds but it just ran away, and I haven't fared any better.'

'You can always get a job. There's more to life than hunting and fishing.'

'A job doing what? I'm not travelling the world like you

do, Edgar, I'm done with foreign parts. I saw more than enough of it during the War.'

'No, but there'll be something for you, Lennox. Something to turn that erratic mind of yours towards.' He leaned back in his chair. 'And I'll buy you an abacus for Christmas; you can learn some accounting – that'll keep you occupied.'

'God forbid,' I replied with feeling. 'And if my resources are depleted thanks to Kingsley, just think what Uncle's fortune has suffered. Peregrine's been his adviser for years – managing the Melrose estate has been pretty much his sole source of income ever since I can remember.'

'And how many times have we advised Uncle to get rid of Kingsley, and has he ever taken the slightest notice of anything you or I say?'

'He takes notice,' I retorted. 'He agrees to get rid of Kingsley every time we mention it – and then carries on exactly as before.'

Edgar nodded. 'Look. Enough talk of finances. Christmas is coming, and we're going to celebrate Uncle's nuptials.' His eyes lit up. 'And there's something else I wanted to tell you.'

'What?'

'It's on the QT, but as you're going to be my best man I feel I should give you due warning.'

'Ha! Don't tell me some lucky lady has got to you too! Who is it – that pretty piece you met in Madrid?'

'No.'

'Rome?'

'Not her either.' Edgar shook his head.

'The Welsh one?'

'Nope.'

'Have I met her?'

'Not yet.'

'Just tell me, or we'll be here all damn night.'

'I will!' Edgar grinned. 'But remember we're holding off the announcement until the new year – we don't want to steal Uncle's thunder.'

'So come on, man, who is she?'

'The Countess's niece – Miss Natasha Czerina Orlakov-Palen.'

CHAPTER 4

I opened my mouth to stutter something, had second thoughts and closed it again as the door opened. We turned in our chairs by the fire, then jumped to our feet. Cooper stepped in to announce the entrance of the arrivals, began to speak, and was instantly drowned out.

'Darlink!' Countess Sophia Androvich Zerevki Polyakov exclaimed loudly, arms held wide and heading straight toward Edgar; then she stopped in her tracks when she saw me. 'Ah, you must be the romantic one! Heat'cliff.' She peered short-sightedly up at me. 'So handsome!' She turned to Uncle Charles, eclipsed at her side. 'Darlink, you didn't told me he vas so handsome!' She smiled widely, cheeks dimpling: a short, dynamic dumpling of a woman with dark hair in a high bun and small bright eyes – she looked like a squirrel who's discovered all the nuts.

'Ah, yes, yes, my little lambkin.' Uncle Charles looked at her adoringly. 'He's a dear boy. Do you remember I told you he was in the War? Aeroplanes, you know, shot down all sorts of bad hats. I mean the Boche. Germans,' he added in a loud whisper.

'Countess.' I bowed, a bit bemused, not to mention relieved that she didn't seem to know me. She raised her outstretched hand to be kissed in the proper fashion. 'Enchanted to meet you,' I said. I was about to add congratulations upon her engagement into the family when she took me unawares and yanked me into an embrace. She barely reached my shoulders but had a bear-like grip, and at close quarters her perfume was overpowering – I'd probably stink of it all night now.

Then, loosening her grasp, the Countess turned on Edgar, who'd had experience of her energetic greeting and accepted it with valour.

'Charlie, I have you, and I have now two handsome young men for my family, with darlink Natasha. My heart it is full,' the Countess declared fortissimo, with ringed hands held over her fulsome bosom.

I exchanged looks with Edgar, brows silently raised. The Countess chattered non-stop as we ensured that she was comfortably seated nearest the hearth, and then arranged ourselves politely in her firing line. The virtual monologue continued; I think it was about a Russian Prince she'd met in Paris. I lapsed back in my chair watching the performance and pondering what to make of it all. It wasn't that I'd done the Countess wrong, quite the reverse, but how was I supposed to tackle such an affair without upsetting any number of delicate sensibilities? And it would have to be tackled some time, because strung around her plump neck was my mother's hideous ruby and diamond necklace.

While I maintained an enthralled expression and churned the puzzle over in my mind, Edgar kept glancing towards the door, presumably waiting for Natasha to arrive. That was another peculiar episode; what was the encounter I'd overheard between Natasha and Kingsley about? Another eggshell incident, and probably politic to keep my mouth shut on that subject too.

Countess Sophia was quite a spectacle, far more animated than I'd expected having envisaged her as a sort of Grand Dame likely to look down her high-bred nose at us provincial gentry. She was gaily expounding on something amusing, arms waving around, rings and bangles flashing, the frills of her orange silk frock flouncing with her movements, while Uncle stared at her with the expression Mr Fogg adopts while waiting for a dog biscuit.

Cooper made another entry and solemnly pronounced, 'Miss Natasha Czerina Orlakov-Palen.'

Edgar jumped to his feet. 'Natasha!' he exclaimed. 'My dear! Let me introduce you to my cousin, Lennox.' Edgar took her hand as Natasha glided in, dusky-rose-coloured silk dress in the modern straight-cut style to the knee, rippling as she moved. She nodded her head gracefully to her aunt and Uncle Charles, her dark hair in a simple chignon and a single string of pearls around her slim neck.

I was on my feet as fast as Edgar – now here was a girl of a very superior cut. I took her proffered hand and kissed it lightly as she gave a slight curtsey.

'Enchanted to meet you, Miss Orlakov-Palen. Edgar has given me some very good reports of you. I understand you have become very close.' This was as much as I could say to drop a hint that I knew about the engagement.

The girl took the cue and smiled from me to Edgar. 'Ah –' she looked up with intelligent grey eyes '– I'm so pleased he has spoken with you.' Her English was nicely enunciated, with only a light accent, and very pleasant to the ear.

Edgar settled Natasha down next to the Countess and retreated to his chair by the fire from where he could gaze at her; I was beginning to feel like a damned gooseberry with all the romance in the air, so I retreated to an over-stuffed chair further away from them all and put my feet up on a stool. A footman was pulling the curtains against the dark, in which I could see more snow was falling; if this kept up, there'd be no chance of fishing or doing anything tomorrow.

Cooper had remained in attendance and was pouring sherry, brandy or whatnot for the assembled, when the door opened and Peregrine Kingsley sauntered in, followed by his son, Adam, and a pale young woman trailing behind them – bloody Kingsleys in duplicate, I thought; just what we needed to make the ensemble complete.

'Ah, you're all here! Excellent!' Adam did the rounds with the sofa crowd and offered a cheery wave to Edgar and me. I ignored him and went to introduce myself to his wife – a drippy woman with mousy hair in a plait wound around her head, and thin rounded shoulders supporting a grey frock that looked as if it had been designed by a curtain-draper.

'Gertrude, how delightful to meet you.' I tried my most charming smile, lifting her limp wrist to my lips, which she barely let hang before drifting away to the group by the fire without so much as raising her eyes or muttering a hello.

Peregrine Kingsley kept his distance, so it wasn't all bad, but Adam bustled over and drew up an armchair next to me, rubbing his hands together. Cooper asked what he'd like to drink and then had to take quite some time finding the very best brandy the house possessed.

'Why are you wearing two wristwatches?' I asked him.

'Very observant of you, old boy, always said you were a clever cove.' He flicked out his wrist to reveal two large shiny gold watches. 'Got a spare, actually; fell in lucky on a deal and the chap had to hand over his ticker in lieu of a debt. Are you in the market? I can give you a good price, you won't get better in the London emporia you know. Mark my words!' Adam grinned like a cat. He had his father's tan and features apart from darker hair, and was dressed, if anything, even more expensively.

'No. Go away.' I waved at Cooper for a top-up brandy, but he was now entirely taken up by the Countess and His Lordship and didn't notice.

'Got a nice set of diamond earrings, if you want to give a gift to one of the gals?'

'Clear off, Adam. I'm not buying anything.'

'Bit short, old boy?' So he had guessed. 'I can let you have a monkey at eight per cent compound. A monkey is five hundred quid, if you don't know the cant.' He winked.

I got up, stalked over to the sideboard and poured my own damned drink, then found a sofa nearer Edgar, who was still gazing at Natasha from a wing chair by the fire.

'Edgar.' No response. 'Edgar!' I had to shout, and everyone turned to look at me for a moment, then went back to their conversations, the hum of noise in the room growing louder as the Countess regaled her audience with another amusing piece of gossip.

Edgar came over, waving to Cooper for another drink, which was instantly delivered. 'What was Adam trying to stiff you with?'

'Gifts,' I replied. 'Didn't bring any. Forgot. What have you bought?'

'The usual. Silk ties for the chaps and scarves for the ladies, a special jewel for 'Tasha. I've got some spare if you need some. We're given all sorts of trinkets and bits and bobs in our job, come in very handy at this time of year.'

I looked at him. 'Why do they give you trinkets?'

'Just helps smooth the path, that's all. You know, making friends between nations, getting trade moving, keeping the money flowing into state coffers. Diplomatic affairs.'

'I thought you were a spy!'

'Good God, no!' Edgar laughed. 'No money in spying. I'm an attaché – thought you knew. Come to my rooms after breakfast tomorrow and we'll find some nice little goodies for you to stash under the Christmas tree.'

'You still in the Chinese rooms?' I asked.

'Yes, of course, why ask?' Edgar's eyebrows rose.

'Ah, well ...' I started to tell him about my new quarters in the Blue rooms when I was interrupted by a very loud peal of gay laughter from the Countess. 'Ah, but darlink, the most beautiful rubies are to be found in Macedonia. Look –' she lifted the ruby on the necklace '– this is most magnificent. Priceless! A rare ruby from Macedonia. The colour, is it not exquisite?'

All eyes turned to gaze at the stone centred in a cluster of sparkling diamonds. I'd never liked the sickly raspberry colour but was quite aware of the value and rarity.

'Didn't your mother used to have one like that, Lennox?' Sir Peregrine asked, regarding me as a cobra eyes a rat.

'Yes, now that I come to think about it, I recall a necklace like that one, too,' Uncle Charles put in. 'Your dear mother often wore it,' he added. 'And I believe it was Russian.'

All eyes turned to me, waiting for an answer.

'Major Lennox!' The Countess suddenly shouted out, pointing at me. 'It is the name! Lennox! I only made think of Heat'cliff – but Lennox. You are the man ...'

She was interrupted by my breaking into a terrible paroxysm of coughing.

'Mustn't call him Heathcliff, my dear. Upsets him, you know,' Uncle confided loudly to her. 'Hard to remember, I know, but there you are, just doesn't like it.'

'Dinner is served,' Cooper announced, and hit the brass gong that he held in his hand with a small hammer.

CHAPTER 5

We followed Uncle Charles as he led his fiancée by the arm from the drawing room to the dining room; we all heard her voice, which carried quite distinctly.

'But Charlie, this I must tell you. About Heat'cliff, the ruby necklace …'

'Yes, yes, my dear.' Uncle Charles patted her hand as they walked slowly down the stairs. 'But I am formally announcing our engagement tonight, and I don't want to forget my speech. Tell me about it later, my lambkin.'

Uncle took his seat at the head of the table with the Countess next to him, then Edgar and the Kingsleys. As heir presumptive I always sat at the opposite end, for which I gave silent thanks: I was keen to keep as far away from the Countess and the subject of ruby necklaces as possible.

Natasha was seated to my left, and the dreary Gertrude on my right, so I felt pretty safe for the moment.

'Did the Countess say that she wants to speak to you about rubies?' Natasha immediately asked.

I stopped sipping my wine for a moment. 'No, no, must have misheard.'

'I think she did,' Natasha added.

I swiftly turned the subject. 'What was Russia like?'

She looked at me closely. 'Terrible. They murdered my parents and tried to kill us. We ran away with almost nothing.'

'Ah, yes, yes ... sorry. Must have been awful, like the War. That was pretty dreadful ... everyone died, you know.' Damn it, I was babbling again.

Soup was served, cold as usual; but the bread was still warm. I looked around for someone to deflect the conversation, but there was only Gertrude, and she didn't seem to be listening never mind joining in; she just sat huddled over her soup, slurping, her eyes flitting sideways towards the top of the table.

I turned back to Natasha and tried a new direction. 'Do you hunt?'

Natasha's eyes lit up. 'On horses? Yes, I much like to ride. I am very good horsewoman.'

'Edgar and I usually ride out after Christmas. New Years Day Hunt and all that. We could all go – plenty of old hacks in the stables. Need the weather to buck up a bit, of course – too much snow will put the kibosh on it.'

'Pooh, it is nothing, this little snow.' She dismissed it with a wave of her hand. 'In Russia we have it up to our legs, it makes plenty of snow, and we need many peasants to dig it away, then we can ride and drive our troika. This I miss very much. I would like one here, perhaps there are artisans who can make one? I think it will be very fine.'

'Ah yes, well, I'm sure someone can, but the weather

isn't very reliable, the snow I mean. Tends to come and go.'

She looked at me with a puzzled frown, then turned to Gertrude. 'Do you like to ride?'

Gertrude looked up suddenly from her soup, her spoon poised. 'No,' she replied almost in a whisper. 'But I like shooting things. Dead,' she said with a grim finality.

We looked at each other, I pulled a face of mock horror and Natasha giggled. Her eyes sparkled when she laughed, and her face lit up. She looked rather beautiful actually.

'Your aunt has made quite a hit with my uncle,' I remarked.

The smile faded from Natasha's face. 'Sophia is remarkable. She makes the hit wherever she goes,' she replied rather coolly.

I guessed Aunty may not be the best topic, but I seemed to be running out of subjects. 'You speak excellent English.' Oh God, that was limp – I am hopeless at talking to women – what the hell is one supposed to say to them?

'We had private tutors. I speak four languages, all very well. I have first-class education. I was invited to attended university in Petrograd to study science and medicine, but I did not choose to go.'

'Really? How extraordinary! Are girls educated in Russia?'

'Of course.' She looked at me in puzzlement. 'The Tzar was an enlightened monarch. Education is the good of the country, good for Russia. Now the peasants rule and no one is educated, people are reduced to ignorant slaves. How many languages do you speak?'

'Um. One, actually. This one.'

Natasha looked around at the umpteen footmen dashing in and out with dishes of food to and from the table. 'There are not many servants in this house. Is Lord Melrose poor?'

I looked around. 'No, I don't think so. I mean, probably not. Seem to be plenty of servants to me, same as usual anyway.' I'd never given it much thought, but there must be at least thirty in the house, which seemed plenty considering they only had to look after one doddery old man.

'Sophia likes a lot of servants, she will have many more than this. We had a hundred in every house we owned in Russia and many more outside. But they were just peasants,' she added dismissively.

'Did she live with you?'

She looked at me with intelligent eyes under finely arched brows; beneath the exterior she was somewhat haughty – aristocratic in the traditional sense.

'Please explain?' she asked.

'You said "we had a hundred in every house". I assumed by "we" you meant your aunt too?'

She regarded her dinner of breast of pheasant, sliced venison, swede, carrots and thick gravy before answering. 'Yes, she did live with us.'

'Did you escape together? Must have been terrifying.'

She nodded. 'There were many soldiers, although they

weren't real soldiers, they were thugs and ruffians from the town. The peasants joined in with the soldiers. Our peasants! They turned on us, they stole our possessions, burned our houses …' She became a little breathless. 'My parents were slaughtered, our guards ran away – the miserable cowards. Sophia saved me. We had to pretend we were servants to escape from our own country.' Her face became rigid and intense with anger.

'I'm sorry,' I said. 'Shouldn't have asked.' Idiot, I thought, next time just stick to the blasted weather.

Natasha turned back to her food, and I glanced at Gertrude, who was eating noisily and still staring at the Countess. I followed her gaze and realised that it wasn't in fact the Countess but the ruby necklace she was so engrossed in. And there was someone else at the table who seemed preoccupied: Peregrine Kingsley was watching Natasha the way Mr Fogg watches me while I'm eating the last morsel of food on my plate and haven't offered him so much as a crust. Whatever had happened between them had affected him far more deeply than it had affected Natasha, it seemed.

'How many peasants are there?' Natasha asked.

'What?'

'Outside – how many peasants does Lord Melrose possess?'

'Um … We don't call them peasants, and no one possesses them nowadays. Democratic, you see: can't own people, not in this country. Not done.'

'Then what are they called? Yokel? I have heard this

word.' The girl raised her elegant brows in question while toying with her meal.

'Farmers – we call them farmers. They get upset if anyone calls them peasants or yokels. Best to remember that, old girl. Could cause a to-do, you know.'

She frowned at me; I could see her assimilating the information. She was bright and quick, just needed some direction in the subtleties of the English class system. And the food – I noticed she hadn't eaten very much of it.

Uncle began banging a spoon at the top of the table and got to his feet as Cooper dashed around filling up each guest's glass in anticipation of the toast.

'My dear family and friends,' Uncle began, and then mumbled on for some time about happiness and dear Sophia and wedding parties. My mind drifted away, wondering if the snow would stop me taking my gun into the woods tomorrow, because fishing was certainly off. Everyone else was staring at Uncle, except Gertrude. Her hand crept onto the table, she wrapped her fingers around her knife and drew it into her lap, where I saw her drop it into her large handbag. That made me sit up all right. I looked around the table – no one else had noticed. Then she did the same with a fork. Bloody hell, she was stealing the silver!

Suddenly everyone started clapping; I guessed Uncle must have made the formal announcement, so I joined in the applause, still watching Gertrude.

This time she snaffled a spoon! I saw her do it, right under everyone's noses. I stared at her – maybe she was the source of Adam's spare watches and whatnots? Were they in it together? Should I say something?

Natasha leaned forward, looking very severe, and quietly snapped, 'Gertrude!'

That did the trick. Gertie closed her bag, clutched it in both hands and scowled at Natasha. I looked on in dumb silence – damned strange bunch of women we seem to have acquired in the family.

Meanwhile, the formalities were still going on. There was a toast, then another, then the Countess stood up. 'My family.' She laughed loudly. 'Now I have a family to my own. I am to become Lady Sophia Melrose! Heat'cliff, Edgar and my little Natasha, I vill be like mother to you all. You do not have no one no more and now it vill be me,' she thrust her champagne glass into the air for emphasis and covered her heart with her other hand. We politely applauded. 'Dear Charlie –' she bent to kiss the wispy curls on his head '– ve vill be too happy. Ve vill all be too happy!'

She burbled on for another twenty minutes: couldn't wait for the big day … only one week away … I rested my chin on one hand and closed my eyes – then snapped them open. A week away? Were we all expected to hang around here for a whole week waiting to attend the wedding? I broke out in a sweat – I'd have to invent some excuse. Greggs dying or something.

Uncle rose to his feet again. 'My dear family, tomorrow is the beginning of our traditional Christmas at Melrose, which we will celebrate together along with our new family members.' He waved vaguely toward his affianced and Natasha. 'I beg you all, please, do not be late for the gift exchange at six o'clock. As usual, Cooper will sound the gong fifteen minutes before the time to remind you to make your way with your gifts to the Christmas tree in the hall.' He sat down, then struggled back up and banged his spoon again, his voice now noticeably more feeble. 'I forgot about dinner. We will have a cold collation because the servants will be holding their annual Christmas feast, so it will just be us, with Cooper on hand, of course. It is best not to ring the bells for the servants after five o'clock as they will all be in the Servants' Hall and we must allow them to enjoy their festival undisturbed.'

Uncle turned to leave the table. I got up hastily and followed the men out while Cooper escorted the ladies to the drawing room for sherry and whatnot.

Adam fell in beside me. 'I say, old boy, got a few solid tips for you. Heard you were a bit –'

'Going for my dog.' I peeled off before he managed to say anything more, and headed downstairs.

Kitchens are the warmest place in any house – no idea why we don't have some sort of stove in normal rooms to sit around. It's always the same in English houses: roasting front, freezing back, most of the heat going straight up the chimney. I asked one of the footmen where stoves were available for purchase, but he said he hadn't got a clue. Mr Fogg was very snug, the maids told me what a wonderful little doggie he was. We gave him treats then

I took him outside into the rapidly falling snow for a pee and a poop, and then we raced upstairs, where the men had finished drinking port and were joining the ladies once again in the drawing room.

'Oh no, no, no. Heat'cliff. This dog, he cannot be in the house,' the Countess shouted as we walked in.

That rather stunned me. 'What?'

'I am mistress nearly now. I do not like the dogs. No more dogs, I am decided.' She closed her small red mouth firmly.

Uncle Charles looked like a startled hare. 'But lambkin –'

He was instantly silenced by a frosty look from his betrothed. 'No, Charlie, no dogs. He can go to the kennels vith the hounds. This and other rules must be changed, darlink, this is not how ve order our houses in Russia.'

'What?'

'Take. Take.' She waved her hand imperiously. 'No dog, take him avay.' She turned to Cooper and clapped sharply. 'You, you are butler. You take him. You do as I say, instant.'

Cooper looked aghast and froze into confounded immobility; a number of jaws dropped, including mine.

The Countess continued: 'Cooper, you are too slow. Too slow for to be man of the household. You vill go too if you do not speed up. Go another house, and ve get good man, young, not old man like you.'

The atmosphere could be cut with a knife. Cooper turned pale; the two footmen standing against the walls were bending forward the better to hear, their eyes wide with shock. Uncle started stuttering again but received another stern glare.

I stooped to pick up Fogg before things got worse.

'I'll take him to my rooms,' I told them. Not much else I could do really, so I left with my dog and a heavy heart.

I relit the oil lamp and read for a while, then thought about the day's strange events. Fogg slept on my bed as usual where he'd made a nest for himself in the thick quilt, and eventually I dropped into troubled slumber.

Bright sunshine, sparkling off snow against the windowpanes and sills woke me early. I got up, my breath white in the cold air, and lit the fire, which had expired in the chill damp. Usually a maid or minion came early to set it alight, but I beat them to it this morning. Once the fire was merrily blazing I pulled on a tattered old dressing gown over my pyjamas and set off to let Foggy out.

We were dashing back upstairs as Cooper was bringing the first tea-tray to His Lordship's guests. Judging by the red rose in the slim vase, the Countess was to be served first.

'I'll have mine in my rooms, Cooper,' I told him in passing. 'Not coming down to breakfast today.'

'Certainly, sir. I do hope you slept well, sir.'

'Pretty well, thank you.'

'Um, sir …'

'What?' I stopped running and turned to face him.

'I have received orders about Mr Fogg. His Lordship had a word with me, as did the Countess – she was quite forceful on the matter, sir.'

'About Fogg? Don't worry, I'll talk to his Lordship myself. And Cooper ...'

'Yes, sir?'

'Don't worry about last evening's outburst, I doubt she meant it; but we'll ensure that a secure place is found for you if necessary.'

Cooper looked grateful but didn't seem convinced by my words. I could sense the tension rising in the household; the servants usually chattered as they went about their work but had fallen silent today. Indeed the house seemed very quiet, as though everyone was holding their breath.

Breakfast was sumptuous but solitary, with only Fogg in attendance. We shared an excellent meal of bacon, eggs, devilled kidneys, crisped bread, sausages, black pudding, toast, honey and butter with a pot of tea. Not being too sure how to handle the delicate situation, I opted for a long tramp in the snow-bound woods to think about it, not even taking my gun, to avoid the distraction. It was quite beautiful, and deathly silent, apart from Fogg barking at the odd pheasant, and sudden thuds as clumps of snow fell from overburdened boughs.

'Blanket.'

Cooper held out the mud-blanket for us on our return, and Fogg was carried off by a nearby footman to the kitchen as usual.

I went in search of Edgar in the Chinese rooms and found him reading the newspaper in a black-, red – and gold-lacquered bed, with a finished breakfast tray next to him.

'Gertie's a kleptomaniac!' I announced.

'I know,' Edgar replied from behind the newspaper.

'Well, you could have said.'

'Haven't seen you all year, old bean. Hardly the sort of thing to put on the back of a postcard, is it?' He folded the paper and put it aside. 'And you didn't go to their wedding.'

'I was fighting a war at the time, Edgar! And why the devil would I go to Adam's wedding? Can't stand him, and nor can you.'

'He has useful contacts.'

'Not for me he hasn't. What does he see in her? She's an absolute wet, not to mention bloody peculiar.' I picked the paper up and then tossed it aside; it was deadly boring, nothing but figures and facts.

'Her father owns an ordnance factory in Yorkshire. He's worth a packet, she'll inherit the lot when he drops off the twig.'

'Stop there.' I held my hand up. 'That explains everything.' I was sitting in a faux bamboo chair by the fire and looked over at him. 'I'm pleased you're marrying for the right reasons, old chap. Natasha seems a bright girl.'

'She's a real find, isn't she!' Edgar grinned broadly. 'We've had some marvellous outings together, you know – museums, the opera, art galleries and such like. She's cultured, educated, intelligent, and a joy on the eye; speaks lots of languages too – she'll make a perfect diplomat's wife.'

'And she'll make you happy?'

'Oh, I'm always happy.' He laughed, eyes lighting up, warming his expression; on the rare occasion that he dropped his guard, Edgar could appear rather calculating.

'The Countess,' I began.

'Fogg,' Edgar countered. 'I know. We were all a bit stunned by her outburst. Uncle tried reasoning with her after you'd gone, but she's a very determined woman. I don't think she's going to change her mind, Lennox.'

My shoulders slumped a little, but I straightened up; no point in letting some minor prejudice get between family. 'I'll keep him out of the way, in my rooms and the kitchens, that should do it.'

'Not the kitchens, old man – Cooper's on thin ice as it is. If the Countess gets wind of it she may give him his marching orders then and there,' Edgar warned.

'Very well, I'll confine him to my rooms,' I replied, feeling somewhat bleak and thinking I'd better go and recover him from his warm spot next to the stove.

'Good plan – and warn the staff. Don't want to upset the old man with a contretemps over Christmas, nor in the run-up to his nuptials next week.'

'Agreed,' I said, 'but we must save Cooper. You could adopt him?' I suggested. 'You know, for your new household with Natasha. Once you're married you'll need to run a real home, not this peregrinatory lifestyle you've been leading. And Cooper could butler for you.'

He stared at me as though I'd lost my mind.

'What?' I asked.

'Lennox,' he started, then paused, as though trying to put the right words together. 'You have a very loose grasp on reality sometimes. You know that I cannot gain access to any part of my fortune until I produce legitimate children, don't you?'

'Yes, you've always made a joke about it. Known about it since your old Pops shuffled off the coil.'

'And until then how do you think I survive?'

'On your earnings, which you said was fine. "Satisfying" was the exact word, if I recall.'

'And entirely inadequate – working for His Majesty's Government wouldn't pay for a Savile Row suit, never mind the upkeep of an apartment in Eaton Square.'

'Doesn't it?'

'Not remotely.' His face suddenly dropped; he looked haggard, the high cheeks pale and lean, those finely sculpted lips drawn in a hard line. 'I'm in debt, Lennox, as deep as you are. I need to unlock the funds soon, or I'm going to be in trouble, too. Do you understand?'

I nodded dumbly. Bloody hell, even Edgar was up to his eyes in it. So much for lecturing me on high finance.

Having made his confession, he tossed the bedcovers aside abruptly and got up to pull on a Chinese silk dressing gown with embroidered dragons and peculiar flowers. 'Don't worry about Gertie, Adam collects all her booty and returns it, it's just a little eccentricity she has.' He frowned, then forced a grin. 'Now, talking of booty, let's get some trinkets for you to hand out. It's Christmas Eve – we exchange gifts tonight, so you can't leave it any longer.'

He had a remarkable number of fancy whatnots: silk ties, cravats, drop pearl earrings, cashmere scarves, leather-bound notebooks and at least half a dozen fine-looking fountain pens. We chose something for each of the relevant parties including all the Kingsleys, despite my objections.

With a feeling of relief that these tiresome festive obligations were complete, I took the back stairs to the kitchens and found a maid to wrap them up while I filched a biscuit to share with Fogg, who was still drying off by the stove. I returned to my room with my dog at my heels and tossed the gifts onto the bed until it was time for the present-giving.

The lunch gong sounded. My long walk through the woods and chat with Edgar had left me decidedly peckish, and I headed to the dining room with a clap of the hands and an appetite worthy of the cook's best efforts.

'Ah, Heat'cliff,' the Countess greeted me upon my entrance. She was sitting in Uncle's chair; Edgar, Peregrine Kingsley and Adam Kingsley were also in attendance and seated around the table. There was no sign of lunch or even a drink.

'Lord Melrose is not vell. I have informed him he vill stay in his bed this day, he must be vell tonight for the present-giving.' She looked up at me over gold-rimmed pince-nez fixed on her nose, her Russian accent heavier than usual.

'Right, fine,' I replied, wondering what was going on.

'Sit down,' she ordered. 'This is a talk of much serious business.'

'Right,' I sat in my usual chair and looked at the others, who were studying their hands for the most part, though Edgar raised his head to wink at me.

'Your Uncle, he is changing his vill,' she said blankly. The sparkly eyes and bright smile had vanished, she was very serious and very Russian at that moment; even her clothes were subdued in shades of russet with cream lace, no gaudy silk in sight. 'He leaves all to me. But von day, Heat'cliff, you vill be Lord Melrose, so you vill be happy.'

That brought a frown to the brow. I had never wanted Melrose Court or its encumbrances, but it seemed a bit off for the Countess to be commandeering the goods and chattels belonging to our family – especially since she and Uncle weren't even married yet.

'Natasha has told me your news, Edgar, and you do not need money, you have plenty of yourself from your rich papa. So you vill be happy too.' She smiled at him, a smile straight from the Steppes.

Edgar stared back evenly at her; he kept his counsel but had a look of steel in his eyes that I recognised as being distinctly dangerous.

'I tell you this now so ve can start our new family with all this thing clean on the table. It is for the best.' There was a stack of yellowed papers in front of her; she kept plucking at them with pudgy fingers glittering with rings. I realised the documents were quite old: vellum and thick linen paper scribed by hand in faded ink, set with red-wax seals and ribbons made long ago. My heart gave a bit of a lurch; those were our family papers, handed down the ages through long generations of Melroses and Lennoxes.

Peregrine chipped in. 'I have drawn up all the new documents and wills as you and His Lordship have requested, Countess Sophia. They are merely awaiting Charles's signature.' He turned and smirked at Edgar and me.

'This vill be tonight ven he signs them, after the gift-opening. Is good idea huh?' She laughed merrily.

'Gertrude and I will act as witnesses,' Adam said. 'And you can rest assured, Countess Sophia, that the Kingsley family will give you all our support and direction during our joint futures together.'

'Absolutely, we are your faithful servants, Ma'am,' Peregrine added, then got to his feet with a smug grin and made a half bow.

Edgar and I exchanged glances – this was outrageous, the Kingsleys were proving even more treacherous than usual, and there wasn't any damn lunch either.

'Ah, but this is not right,' the Countess said to Peregrine.

'Sorry?' he replied, eyebrows arched, 'I don't understand.'

'You vill not give advices to me. I am having new lawyer, a good Russian. You and you –' she pointed to father and son '– I vill not need. This is finished.' She slapped one hand down on the stack of documents and turned to me with a cold stare. 'Heat'cliff. You come to see me in the morning at ten of clock, I vill talk vith you here in this room.'

She nodded imperiously at me, then waved us all away.

I stood up, swiftly followed by Edgar. Kingsley father and son remained in their seats, their slack mouths falling open and closed before shutting with a snap, and both of them looking furious.

'Ha,' I laughed. 'You've been put out to grass, Kingsley!'

At least the whole palaver ended on a high note.

CHAPTER 6

'I suppose I should have seen it coming,' Edgar said in the Melrose Arms not a mile away from the house. We'd motored down in the Bentley after the Countess's bombshell, looking for lunch and liquid consolation. Foggy had come with us, he was snoring at our feet in front of the fire while we leaned on a battered table with a frothing pint of beer each. We sat under low ceilings with blackened beams near the old pews set along the walls where snow-damp locals in various states of inebriation had greeted us. The smell of woodsmoke, spilt beer, malt, stale tobacco, wax polish, wet dogs and local farmers filled our nostrils – a blissful state of affairs if it hadn't been for that unpleasant encounter still ringing in our ears.

'Well, I never saw it coming – never even dreamed it, actually,' I replied. 'And she didn't even wait until she had a ring on her finger.'

'She had a huge one, that diamond could double as a bloody beacon,' Edgar contradicted between sips of beer. We were both dressed in country tweeds – his much smarter than mine through lack of daily use.

'Yes, but that's just an engagement ring, she's not his wife yet,' I pointed out.

'Understand this, Lennox, if Uncle called it off she'd bring a suit for breach of contract. Once he'd made the formal announcement last night, she had him in the bag. And he's an honourable man, he's not going to cry off, so don't even consider that line of thought.'

I let out a long breath. 'It isn't the money or the house, Edgar, it's the family history. We were brought up on it – it meant something, or it did to me anyway. You know, continuity and all that,' I tried to explain, then looked at him. 'Will it affect your plans?'

'No, I can't change anything,' he said quietly, then changed tack. 'Why does she want to see you?'

'Haven't a clue,' I lied – my turn to change the subject. 'Do you think she'll make Uncle happy?'

Edgar paused, staring at his pewter tankard and rubbing his thumb across dribbles of beer that trickled down its side. 'I did think so.' He paused. 'I'm not so sure now.'

'Thought your job depended on judging people.' I tried to josh him but his mood was low and he frowned at me.

'I was too optimistic, seeing what I wanted to see. I won't make that mistake again.' He took a long draught of beer, draining his tankard, then raised it in the air to be refilled by the barmaid.

'Any plan coming to mind?' I asked after we'd both been topped up.

'Nothing short of shooting her,' he joked, and let loose a cold smile.

A pretty waitress served us with plates piled with green peas, mashed potato and a thick slice of steak pie bubbling with gravy. We tucked in and then spent an hour over a few more pints throwing ideas around before accepting the reality that the Countess had outmanoeuvred us.

We motored back to the old house through drifting snow in a state of gloom. I reached my rooms and started packing; Cooper came in with a pot of coffee and a plate of scones and made a fuss of me, offering to help, acting like my old nurse. We didn't talk about the changes in the house or the new plans, but there was worry in Cooper's eyes, I could see it, and it made me realise that it wasn't just me. So I told Cooper I was staying – least I could do and all that – then we unpacked and put everything away again.

Not knowing what else to do, I sat in the window seat watching the servants scurrying back and forth across the courtyard, making pathways through the ever-deepening snow. A maid carried a bundle of laundry to the wash-house; another took a copper pail to the dairy for milk; a gardener arrived with a dozen dead chickens ready for plucking at the meat store where the butcher did his work. About ten minutes later the cook waddled over and collected them, now plucked and dressed, and fetched them to the kitchen in a large basket on her hip. The house was rather like a small village: everyone had their tasks in return for which lodging, food and fuel and wages were provided, and a benevolent old man was at the head of the pecking-order pyramid. It wasn't so bad a life really, I mused, unless 'benevolent' were exchanged for 'despotic'. Then it would be a very different matter.

There was a knock at the door. Adam came in without waiting to be asked, gave me a broad grin and held out my Montblanc fountain pen.

'That's mine!' I took it from him and peered at it – Gertrude must have pinched it.

'Thought I'd better return it, old boy.' Adam winked, then sat on the bed looking around. 'What on earth are you doing in this dump? There are much nicer rooms in the house. We've got the Italian suite – they're fabulous, there are gold angels on the ceiling, you know.'

'Yes, I do know, Adam. What do you want?' I was in no mood for lawyers.

Adam held his hand up. 'Nothing at all, Lennox, just thought I'd come and offer you my commiserations – looks like the old girl has outsmarted you.'

'Huh.' I moved over to sit in the chair by the fire, which was as far away from him as I could get. 'Could say the same for you and your pa – you two have been fired!'

'You can start a suit, you know. Undue influence and all that.' Adam put on a serious lawyerly face, 'Pa and I, we'll raise the paperwork for you. Might cost a bit, but we'll do it on a loan basis, charge it again this house. You've got nothing to lose, old boy, you're not going to get Melrose Court whatever happens.'

'Adam.' An exasperated sigh escaped my breast. 'Do

you seriously think I'm going to sue my uncle and his fiancée? You really are an absolute snake!'

'Just giving you some friendly legal advice,' Adam replied. 'I'm not even charging you for it. It would cost a fortune, you know, that sort of advice in London.'

'Go away, Adam.'

'Now, there's no need to become vexed, Lennox. I realise it's a sensitive subject, but I'm only trying to help.'

I got up and held the door wide open. 'Out! Now!' I raised my voice for emphasis and Fogg growled his support from under the bed.

'Very well. But don't forget what I said. And that loan, it's a good deal – only nine per cent compound. You won't get better!'

'You said it was eight per cent yesterday.'

'Ah, but that was yesterday.' He went off laughing.

I read for an hour or so, then heard the gong ring three times. This was the order for everyone in the household to come. I closed the door carefully, telling Foggy to stay and be quiet because we didn't need any more drama in the house – not until Christmas was over anyway.

We were all expected to gather beside the Christmas tree in the hall; according to family tradition, gifts were exchanged at six in the evening on Christmas Eve, and the grandfather clock in the corner was creeping towards the hour, so we needed to get a move on. Cooper was standing by with a large steaming punchbowl on the refectory table surrounded by crystal cups. More bunches of holly had been tied to sundry objects, and one of the suits of armour held a bouquet of ivy. Red candles had been lit and placed on myriad stands – it all looked and smelled very festive. I could even hear Christmas carols being sung by the servants downstairs. I tossed my wrapped offerings under the tree and went over to Uncle, who was stationed in front of the hearth, where a massive log had been set ablaze and was roaring merrily away.

'Greetings, Uncle Charles.' I gave the old man a hug. He was wearing his purple velvet smoking jacket, a matching embroidered cap over his white hair, and looking very natty.

'Good evening, my dear boy,' he greeted me with a tremor in his voice. 'Now, don't you worry about a thing. I'm sure Sophia didn't mean it about your doggie.' He looked up at me anxiously. 'You're not going to leave, are you?'

'No, Uncle, of course not.' I fixed my best smile for him by way of reassurance. 'Where is the lovely lady, by the way?'

'Oh, no doubt she'll be down soon. I don't know what they do in Russia at Christmas. Do you think they celebrate it too?'

'No idea, we can ask Natasha, she's coming down now.'

Natasha had a colourful paper bag full of presents in her hand which she emptied and arranged carefully under the tree before coming to kiss Uncle warmly, and then turned to extend her hand to me. I played the gallant and bent over it with a brief bow.

'Good evening to you –' she smiled radiantly '– and may I wish you a very happy Sochelnick.'

'Ah, is that what you call it?' Uncle rejoined, laughing. 'Sokelnick! Happy Sokelnick!'

'It is Sochelnick, but you say it very goodly,' she replied, laughing down at him and holding both his hands.

'Happy Schlolzzlenick,' I wished her merrily. Her laughter was infectious, something had cheered her up, she was positively glowing – perhaps Edgar was going to make their announcement tonight?

Uncle Charles kept hold of her hands and started to ask her about Russian festivities as Edgar came down grinning, threw his gifts upon the growing pile of goodies, and the hugging started all over again.

I drifted over to Cooper guarding the punchbowl and asked for a large one. I was emptying it when Adam and his drippy wife arrived and made the rounds shaking hands. Gertrude dropped off their gifts while eyeing the gaily wrapped boxes under the tree.

'Should have put a guard on that lot,' I said sotto voce to Edgar.

'I did.' He nodded toward a footman standing unobtrusively at the back of the hall.

Ha! That made me laugh.

'Your dog's running round in the upstairs corridor, old boy,' Adam informed me with a grin.

That wiped the smile off my face. 'Nonsense, he's shut up in my room.'

'Your dog is making a lot of noise in the corridor upstairs.' Sir Peregrine Kingsley came sauntering down with a stack of parcels held ostentatiously in his arms and placed them under the tree. 'You should keep him locked up. The Countess will be very displeased.'

It wasn't possible for Foggy to have escaped – damn it, should I go and check? If I did, Uncle would be terribly upset at my messing up our traditional gift exchange; on the other hand, his fiancée would probably be livid if Fogg were indeed loose.

The grandfather clock started to strike six, and all eyes turned to the staircase in anticipation of the Countess's entrance. Mr Fogg suddenly came bounding down, wagging his tail excitedly.

'Told you, Lennox,' Peregrine Kingsley drawled.

'Oh hell! Excuse me, Uncle.' I took off after him. 'Come here, Fogg. How the devil did you get out?' The dog, thinking it was a fine game, dashed back upstairs with me in hot pursuit, then raced along the passage into the drawing room, and suddenly ran out again with his tail down.

'Damn it, come here Fogg!'

A loud bang sounded as I neared the open door, followed by a billow of smoke. I ran to the threshold, wondering what had caused it, then entered. There was a blast of cold air and black smoke in the room, although this was clearing quickly, dispersed by the draught from one of the sash windows, which for some reason was wide open. That's when I realised somebody was lying on the floor in front of the fire. I walked over – it was the Countess, lying flat on her back staring at the ceiling, her arms akimbo.

I leaned over her – she was strangely reminiscent of the fat man who had been lying in a very similar position only three days ago. I looked at her face and the trickle of blood running down the side of it.

Bloody hell, she'd been shot!

I froze stock-still, astounded, and remained there for a good few seconds trying to make sense of it. There was something just under the edge of her red silk dress, and I bent down to get a closer look: it was the handle of a gun, with an ivory grip – it looked just like my pocket pistol. I reached over her body to pick it up, when a noise from the doorway made me spin around; it was everyone from downstairs, and they were staring at me with their mouths wide open.

'Lennox,' Uncle cried, 'what have you done?'

CHAPTER 7

I stared, they stared back. Then I remembered the gun in my hand and dropped it like a hot poker. An explanation was required – rather urgently required. I opened my mouth to provide one, but nothing came out, so I closed it.

Uncle tottered a bit, raised a pointing finger at me, then at the body of his ex-affianced, and back at me again. With a ghastly pallor on his face he seemed to shrink; Cooper took him by the arm and led him slowly away.

'Lennox, what the hell have you done?' Edgar asked, with considerably more force than Uncle had managed. He stalked over, dropped a handkerchief over the pistol, carefully wrapped it and put it in his pocket.

I shook my head, looking down at the lifeless body of the Countess sprawled on the rug, and shook it again. 'Nothing,' I coughed, my voice feeling strangulated. 'She was like this. I mean, I found her like this.'

Then Natasha added more drama to the scene by letting out a piercing shriek and falling to the floor. Edgar tried to catch her but missed; he knelt beside her clutching her hand, then picked her up in his arms and carried her away, shouting for smelling salts and a doctor.

'I'm calling the police.' Peregrine Kingsley announced. 'Lennox, you ... you ... murderer,' he shouted at me, and ran off down the stairs.

Adam came closer to take a better look. 'You need a good lawyer, old chap. I can give you excellent rates, don't you worry!' He rubbed his hands together in anticipation of the fees, then turned to follow his father.

I wanted to hit him, but nothing would move, I was fixed to the spot in a sort of shocked paralysis.

That's when Gertrude took a chance and dashed up to the body, leant over making some sort of strange noise, before she too ran out of the room.

What the hell was I meant to do now? I stumbled over to the nearest chair, slumped down and stared – speechless. It didn't make any sense. There was now only me and the corpse left in the room. I needed a drink, so I stood up and made to step over the body, heading for the sideboard, when the footman who'd been guarding the Christmas tree appeared silently in the doorway and took up position at one side of it – Cooper must have sent him up. Clever of him, dear old Cooper, he thought of everything.

I sat down again. What should I do? Think man, I urged myself, get a grip – you've been in tight spots before, it's not like you've got the Boche hammering your tail with a bloody machine gun. I looked at the body – it was hard to miss – strange how she looked even fatter lying there; not as fat as the fat man, of course, but she was still a very plump pudding.

Her eyes had a look of shock about them, probably with good cause in the circumstances. Her small puckered mouth was formed in an expression like an 'O', and her cheeks were round and rosy – whether from the heat of the fire, or rouge, or both, I didn't know.

She wasn't wearing the ruby and diamond necklace, which was odd, as I hadn't seen her without it since I'd met her. Was she wearing it when I found her? Yes … No. Damn it, was she or wasn't she? Gertie could have swiped it if she had been. No! The Countess hadn't been wearing it, and I saw, now, a slight scratch on the side of her neck where it must have been snatched off. Well, that's progress of sorts, my first glimmering of rational thought since I walked in here.

I needed that drink. The footman was watching me round-eyed but didn't seem inclined to actually do anything – I expect this was his first murder, too. I stepped over the recumbent Countess and went to the sideboard to pour a glass of brandy to take back to my chair in front of the fire, stepping carefully over the body as I went. That felt better – so, what should I do now? I peered at her again; she seemed a bit paler than before, although I think we all were. Hardly surprising in the circumstances, I suppose.

What about her rings? Were any of her rings missing? I slid from my seat and knelt down to look at the hand nearest to me. The big diamond engagement ring was still there, and it looked as if the others were, too. She had one on each finger – she wasn't a woman who went in for moderation. All the rings were new, no sign of wear or being overgrown by flesh – unlike my signet ring, which had lost most of its markings and I had to use soap to get it off nowadays. Strange, all the rings being new; she must have owned some in Russia, but they all looked British and modern, not foreign at all.

The rings slipped up and down easily, I didn't have to tug hard to get one off. I took the one from her first finger, turning it over in my hand and examining it closely – bright gold, not even a scratch. Poised to remove another, I realised there was someone in the doorway.

'Harrumph.' A slim man with slicked-back hair and a smart suit under a trench coat was standing watching me with a gimlet eye. I dropped both the ring and the dead hand, which fell with a thump to the floor.

'Chief Inspector Swift,' he intoned.

'Damn!' Was my best response. (Actually, it probably wasn't the best response at all.) I stood up. 'Inspector. Please realise that I didn't do it. Nor the ring – I was checking it … the ring I mean.'

This didn't look good. He stared at me in the same way as the others had, but with more serious intent.

'Not to worry, Major Lennox. We'll soon find out who was responsible. Why don't you sit down and make yourself comfortable.'

Good God, he thinks I'm some sort of lunatic. And babbling didn't help: made me look even guiltier, if that were possible.

'Look,' I tried again, running my fingers through my hair. 'Why don't you ask me some questions? Maybe you can make some sense of it.' I sat down wearily; the day had become very complicated.

Inspector Swift waved away the footman, who was virtually goggle-eyed watching the drama unfold in front of him, and went off looking back over his shoulder as Inspector Swift closed the door firmly behind him.

The Inspector walked slowly into the room looking attentively around, keen brown eyes coming to rest on the body stretched the length of the hearthrug at my feet; then he quickened up, closing in, drawing a pen and notebook from his pocket as he approached. He arrived beside the corpse and stood stock still, observing closely, head slightly to one side, and then he wrote notes in his book, rapidly filling a page with a neat, precise hand.

'Why did you kill the Countess?' he suddenly flung at me.

'I didn't.'

'You did! You were the only one here, it was your gun, everyone heard the shot.'

'Yes. Wait. No.' What was I supposed to say? 'I was set up!' Now, that was something to hang onto because it was true.

'If you'll forgive me, Major Lennox, everybody says that.'

'Do they?'

He nodded, then started writing again. 'What did she say to you before she died?'

'Nothing – she already had.'

'What?'

'Died.'

He eyed me narrowly over the top of his notebook. 'Why did you open the window?'

'I didn't, it was open when I came in.'

'Was she standing up or sitting down when you shot her?'

'I didn't shoot her!'

'Uh-huh.' The Inspector made another careful note. 'Did you argue with her?'

'No! Well, we had a few high words earlier in the day.'

He looked at me as if I were an ant under a microscope. 'About what?'

I was going to have to tell him about the meeting and the will. Damn it, I had the best motive anyone could imagine – someone had indeed set me up, and they'd made a damn good job of it.

There was a sharp rap on the door and a very smartly turned out young sergeant entered, leaving the door open behind him.

'Is that him?' He too stared at me, which was becoming quite annoying; what was I, exhibit A?

'Come in, Sergeant. Major Lennox, this is Sergeant Webb.' We nodded warily at each other, his eyes moving from me to the body.

'She's big, isn't she. Can I 'ave a look, sir?'

'You can, but don't touch anything. Did you take all the statements?'

Sergeant Webb was leaning over the corpse looking into her glassy eyes. 'Certainly did, sir. They all said the same – that gent there shot this woman 'ere.'

'I did not! Has no one heard of being innocent until proven guilty?'

'Now, you sit yourself down, Major Lennox.' The Inspector spoke firmly. 'I'll have the handcuffs on you if you don't behave.' He turned to his sergeant. 'Dust for fingerprints, Webb.'

'Certainly, sir. Shall I take the gentleman's prints, sir?'

'No, we can do that down at the station.'

'What? I'm not going to the station. I haven't done anything.' I protested as Adam turned into the open doorway. 'Clear off, Adam.' He was the last person I wanted to see.

'Have you charged him yet?' he asked. Hands in pockets, he sauntered over to get another look at the body.

'No. And what's it got to do with you?' Inspector Swift asked him.

'I'm his lawyer.'

'No, you're not.'

'Shut up, Lennox. Yes, I am, and I have to inform you, Inspector Swift, that you've only got circumstantial evidence. You can't arrest him.'

'Nonsense, of course I can.'

'No one actually saw him take the shot.'

'It was his gun.'

'Could have been a plant!'

'It was,' I shouted, jumping to my feet.

'Sit down, Major Lennox,' Swift snapped. 'All the

statements agree that everyone was gathered together downstairs in the front hall, including you, sir.'

'The servants weren't, though, were they? You don't know where they were.'

'Yes, I do, they were having Christmas dinner together in the Servants' Hall while the family were opening their presents.'

'All of them?' Adam asked. 'Can you prove beyond doubt that all of them were there?'

Inspector Swift hesitated; Adam laughed.

'Ha, got you!' I shouted and jumped up, pointing at Swift. They both glared at me so I sat down again.

'I can charge him pending further enquiries and arrest him later.'

'Fine. You do that,' Adam told him with a firm nod of the head – I'd have embraced him if he hadn't been such an oily tick.

Sergeant Webb dusted fine grey powder all over the room, brushed off the excess with a shaving brush and examined it through a magnifying glass. Then he picked up bits of hair and heaven knows what else with tweezers, putting them in jam jars – I have to say it looked more Women's Institute than Sherlock Holmes. Finally, he took my prints with smudgy black carbon and escorted me to the smoking room while he and Swift continued their evidence-gathering without me.

I was made to hang about for another hour while they carted out the Countess, which was a drama in itself involving several Constables and much colourful language. I watched them struggle with the stretcher down the stairs until Swift ordered me back to the smoking room. About an hour later he returned and asked more questions. Why was my gun there? Where was the necklace? Why did I kill her? What was the argument about earlier? Eventually, they ran out of steam and read me the charges. It all sounded pretty ominous in legal parlance. Adam had come back by this time and chipped in when it got really sticky. I was made to sign a statement, and by the time I was released it was nearly midnight. I was informed that I was officially under house arrest and warned not to leave Melrose Court or the grounds under any circumstances.

I went back to my rooms, relieved to be still walking the corridors. Adam dogged my footsteps despite my best attempts to lose him.

'That went pretty well if I say so myself,' he said, sounding pretty chipper. 'Don't worry, Lennox, we can drag this out for months. Something might turn up and save your neck from the noose, miracles have been known to happen.' He laughed.

'And you're intending to charge by the hour, I assume?'

'Usual fees, usual terms, old boy.'

'You know, Adam –' I stopped, and turned around to face him '– if I really were a murderer, what makes you think you'd live long enough to collect?'

That wiped the smirk off his face.

CHAPTER 8

I tossed and turned most of the night. Fogg scratched at the door to be let in during the early hours and came to curl up on the quilt next to me – I've no idea where he'd been; the kitchen, probably. I awoke with my mind buzzing, then got up and yanked open the drawer of the bedside locker where I kept my pocket pistol. It was gone. This should not have come as any surprise because it had been used to shoot the Countess and had been left next to her body; but it felt like a shock all the same. It didn't take a genius to work out someone must have been in there, stolen it, and let the dog escape. Then it occurred to me that I shouldn't have touched anything because it may have had fingerprints on it. Damn it, if the police hadn't been so convinced I was guilty they would have thought of this themselves – now I'd probably ruined any evidence of my innocence.

I sat on the bed feeling dispirited; at length Cooper brought in breakfast on a tray. He looked at me sadly, or with disappointment – I wasn't sure which.

'How's Uncle? Lord Melrose, I mean.'

'Taking it rather hard, sir. I haven't seen him so low since Lady Mary passed away. He is keeping to his rooms today, I have been in attendance as much as he will allow.'

'I didn't shoot her, Cooper. I've no idea what the hell's going on, but I didn't shoot the woman.'

'No, sir, I can't imagine you did.' He placed the tray on the table by the fire.

'Will you take Mr Fogg and let him out please, Cooper?'

'Of course, sir, and there are some fine scraps left over in the kitchen for him, too.'

'What's everyone else doing?'

'Mr Edgar is trying to comfort Miss Natasha. Sir Peregrine is taking breakfast in the breakfast room with Mr Adam and his lady wife, sir.'

'No police around, then?'

'No, sir. It's a bit unlikely they would be here today.'

'Why?'

'Because it's Christmas Day, sir. May I wish you a very Merry Christmas, sir.' Cooper gave a short, dignified bow.

Damn, I'd completely forgotten what day it was.

'The same to you too, Cooper,' I replied, without much enthusiasm.

Cooper left with a light step and Mr Fogg gambolling at his heels – at least he didn't have to worry about being sacked now.

Cook had prepared a breakfast fit for a condemned man; it bucked me up no end, and I resumed my seat in the window watching the comings and goings of the staff bustling across the courtyard. Can't say I was much calmer in the cold light of day, but I was becoming more determined. Some blaggard had laid a very clever trap for me, and I'd fallen straight into it – well, I was dashed if I was going to take that lying down.

Must admit, though, half an hour after making the grand plan to track down the perpetrator, I was none the wiser. It couldn't possibly be Uncle, nor Edgar – I'd known and loved them all my days, and neither would be capable of cold-blooded murder. Well. Edgar might, I mused ... but he wouldn't set me up to hang for it. Peregrine and Adam would though; it would be genuinely infra dig on their part, but that didn't mean they weren't capable of it. And the two ladies – Natasha and Gertie? Neither had ever met me before – what possible motive could they have?

I looked down again at the servants dashing along the snowy pathways. There lay the big unknown: was it one of them? And if so, how on earth was I going to find out?

There was no immediate answer that I could see, so I looked around for something I could do and decided it would be a good idea to check the rest of my guns. Everything proved to be present and correct in the cupboard in my dressing room. Examining my collection, I noticed the Mauser was showing signs of a little rust and realised it was quite a long while since I'd cleaned my small arsenal. Not having anything else to occupy myself with, I took all the handguns off their shelves and carried them out, arranging them along the window sill of my bedroom in order to oil and clean them in the pale light of day.

A knock was made on my door just as I was dusting off the single-action Colt 45, a particularly handsome revolver with a very nice blue-grey finish to the steel. I lifted it up to the window the better to check the sights and line of the barrel when Cooper entered with a silver tray bearing a gift and dropped it with a clatter on the doorstep. Poor chap, he really was getting quite old; perhaps the last few days of drama had been too much for him.

I put the gun down and made a fuss of him, picking up the wrapped Christmas present and tray while reassuring him that it wasn't his fault.

'Do you have any particular plans for your guns, sir?' he asked rather breathlessly.

'I'd like to take them out for some practice, Cooper, but I fear it might cause rather a stir if I did.'

'I fear it might, sir,' he agreed.

'I'll just put them away again. Was that a gift for me?'

'Yes, sir. Um, would like me to help you put away the guns, sir?'

'Certainly, Cooper, if you wish. Bring that box over there, would you.' I collected up three gleaming automatics and two revolvers, leaving the mahogany case holding my matching pair of antique duelling pistols to Cooper. We arranged them on shelves below my Purdey shotguns and rows of ammunition, then carefully locked the doors.

'Who's it from?'

'Pardon, sir?'

'The gift. Who's it from?' Poor chap, he really did seem very confused today.

'I was instructed to leave it without a message, sir.'

'How mysterious!' I ripped the wrapping off to reveal a book. It was from Uncle's library, even had dust on it: *The Hound of the Baskervilles* by Arthur Conan Doyle. I smiled and turned over the outer cover to read the inscription on the flyleaf: 'To my dear nephew Heathcliff Lennox – For your further studies, your ever loving Uncle, Charles.' I admit it brought a tear to my eye: despite the death of his fiancée, police running all over the house, a completely ruined Christmas, not to mention the unfounded accusations against his nephew and heir, the old man still believed in me.

'Thank you, Cooper, and please tell Lord Melrose that I wish him a peaceful Christmas and I will see him when he feels strong enough.'

'I will, sir.'

'Oh, and bring me some lunch and Mr Fogg up, would you, I've got some research to do.' I waved the book at him.

'Certainly sir.' Cooper went off, looking a lot chirpier than when he arrived.

I employed the afternoon deep in Sherlock Holmes beside a roaring fire, my dog at my feet, a tray of good festive fare and a bottle of fine brandy at my elbow. Dusk was gathering when I found Uncle Charles dozing in his suite of rooms overlooking the front portico and drive. They were very grand rooms: high ceilings, a regal four-poster bed with all the drapery in the bedroom, the sitting room cluttered with spindly regency furniture gilded and inlaid with colourful fruitwoods, huge tapestries hung upon oak-panelled walls with many excellent oil paintings between them. Uncle seemed a little lost in such a large space, hunched up in his wing chair in front of the marble fireplace, logs crackling away. He'd aged overnight, looked a bit like Methuselah's grandfather, and wasn't even dressed for the day, still being in nightcap, dressing gown and Turkish slippers.

He woke as I entered, and mumbled, rubbing his eyes.

'Merry Christmas, Uncle.' I greeted him cheerfully and held out my gift to him.

'My dear boy,' he smiled gamely. 'Merry Christmas.' He gathered his wits and became sad again. 'What a to-do we've had – quite dreadful.'

I put the gift on his lap and said, 'Thank you for the book.'

'Ah, yes, it was Edgar's idea. Thought it might gee you up a bit.'

'It did,' I replied. 'Not sure that I'm going to dash out and purchase a deerstalker and pipe, but it put the old grey matter to work.'

He unwrapped his present, an old silver-framed photograph of the family back in the day when they were all still alive and breathing. I admit it was the only gift I'd thought to bring from home and I had kept it in my carpet bag until now as I'd wanted to give it to him personally. He gave me a crumpled smile in return and held the gift in his hands, staring at it myopically.

'Want me to find your glasses?'

'No, I know what they look like, I'll remember them as long as I live.' His voice faltered. 'It wasn't you, was it, my boy?'

'No, Uncle, it wasn't.'

'I don't think the police will look at anyone else, Lennox, so it falls to you to unveil the culprit.' He raised his finger and shook it at me. 'You must catch the dreadful person who did this and convince the police of it.'

'I will. I don't know how, but I'll find a way.'

'Good man,' his voice was still tremulous but gaining strength; he'd get through it now – I'd make damn sure he would.

'Sherry?' I proposed.

'Whisky!' he demanded.

We were toasting the family and the future when Edgar came in.

'Ha, this is a fine turn up! Seasons greetings to you, Lennox.'

'And to you, Edgar.' I poured him a glass. 'How's Natasha?'

'Asleep at last. The doctor left a packet of sleeping draughts, and I've finally persuaded her to take one. She's very cut up – as you'd expect. The Countess was her last surviving relative.'

'I'm sorry, Edgar,' I told him, and meant it.

'He didn't do it!' Uncle told him.

'No, probably not. But you'd better find out who did, Lennox, because no one else is going to believe you,' Edgar replied tartly.

We sat beside the fireside in good spirits; Cooper came in and offered to arrange a cosy Christmas dinner for us to eat in the room. An excellent suggestion to which we immediately agreed, so the good butler ordered up two footmen to clear Uncle's large circular reading table. They spread a white linen cloth across it, set it with candles, silver cutlery, the best family porcelain, crystal wine glasses and Christmassy decorated whatnots. Then served we three with an excellent meal of roast goose, sage and onion stuffing, roast potatoes with gravy, chestnuts and sprouts, followed by flaming plum pudding with brandy butter – marvellous! We cleared our plates, quaffed our wine in good humour and finished very content with a toast to our small family being back together again.

'So,' Edgar turned to me as we sipped our port and lit cigars back on our chairs in front of the fire. 'What's your plan? You can't leave things hanging like this, the police will be back in business tomorrow and proving your guilt will be top of their agenda.'

'The gunshot,' I said.

They both looked at me with eyebrows raised.

'You heard it, didn't you? Down in the hall.'

'We did.' Uncle nodded. 'It alerted us to the deed.'

'The pocket pistol is a .22 calibre 642 Smith and Wesson Ladysmith; it could barely be heard outside the room, never mind all the way down the staircase.'

'It was a devil of a bang,' Edgar conceded. 'And it happened just as the Countess was killed. If it wasn't a shot, what else could it have been?'

'I have no idea,' I answered honestly. 'There was a loud retort as I approached the drawing room, and a lot of smoke.' I turned to Edgar. 'First thing tomorrow you must order the police to bring the pistol here and fire it in that room. That will prove that it wasn't the gunshot you heard.'

Edgar laughed.

'What's so funny?' I was rather offended.

'Hearing you actually using your intellect for a change,' Edgar replied. 'You've spent your life hunting, shooting and fishing, and your stint in the War was merely an extension of that. It's about time you found a career.'

'This is not a career,' I snapped.

'Perhaps,' Edgar said, suddenly serious. 'But your life still depends on the outcome.'

We broke up shortly afterwards: Uncle was flagging and in need for an early night, and I rang for Cooper to come and help him to bed. Edgar went off to check on Natasha – I found his devotion was quite remarkable considering how many women he usually had stringing along.

I made my way back through the quiet house and stopped by the drawing room. Someone had locked it and left a large handwritten sign on the door: 'Strictly No Entry. Police Investigation.' I felt for the key on top of the lintel, and let myself in.

I flicked on the lights and looked around. There was grey dust on all of the surfaces; even with the naked eye I could see fingerprint patterns in the powder. What were these supposed to signify? Surely the only prints that mattered were on the pistol?

I went over to the spot on the hearthrug where the Countess had fallen yesterday evening; there was no bloodstain to be seen. Well, I'd shot plenty of game in my time, and untold numbers of Germans during the War (although most of them had been in their own aeroplanes). I'd spent time at the front too; death and corpses were no stranger to me. Whoever had shot the Countess had done so from very close quarters; the gun almost had to be touching the flesh. The hole I'd seen in her temple was small and neat with a ring of gunpowder around it; the bullet would have bored into her brain and she'd have fallen like a stone.

The window which had been open on the night of the murder was now closed, it was a simple sash window which slid up and down aided by a hidden pulley system. There were prolific sprinklings of grey powder on the frame and glass, but I couldn't see any fingerprints at all even after blowing off the excess. I examined all the other windows in the room: they too had been powdered, and all of those frames showed multiple prints. Only the one window lacked them – clear evidence that somebody had wiped the frame clean after opening it.

So what had caused the smoke? Not the pistol – it was far too small, and I kept it loaded with smokeless powder. The only reason the window could have been open was to disperse the smoke from the fire. Fortunately the locked door had prevented the maids from clearing out the hearth, so I was able to poke around in the remains of coal and logs. Beneath the grate there seemed to be a large pool of oil, some of which had soaked into the ashes. I pulled out the base to have a better look. On closer inspection, it proved to be not oil but wax – presumably candle wax, as there were myriad candles in the house.

I prodded the stuff, but it didn't seem to help, so I took a taper from a vase on the mantelpiece and lit it to throw some illumination on it. There were signs that the wax had spattered up the interior of the fireplace and then leaked down through the grate. I couldn't conceive of how a candle could have made a noise like a gun going off, but I was sure it was related. I would insist that Inspector Swift saw this tomorrow.

I locked the door behind me and replaced the key. As I was in the mood for investigations, I stopped by the Christmas tree in the hall to survey the presents still piled under it. There didn't appear to be anything missing: everyone's gifts to each of the other guests were there. Naïvely, I'd rather hoped someone hadn't labelled a gift for the Countess because they knew she was about to be killed. But nothing so simple, of course: the murderer had planned this event carefully and failing to provide a present for the victim would have been an instant give-away.

I rifled through the pile to find the one I'd designated for Adam. It was a very nice leather-bound notebook, which I had thought he could use to keep a list of Gertrude's ill-gotten gains. Given recent events, however, I decided my need was greater than his so I ripped off the wrapping paper, handed it to a footman who was standing around with his mouth open, and took it upstairs to my rooms to jot down some thoughts. I fell asleep with Mr Fogg lying next to me, feeling a great deal more ready to face the Old Bill in the morning.

CHAPTER 9

I breakfasted in my rooms and then sought fresh air with Fogg. Tucking one of my Purdey shotguns under my arm and shoving a pocketful of cartridges in my jacket, we set off for a long tramp through the woods in deep snow hoping to bag a fat pheasant – well, I was hoping to; Fogg's dislike of the dead would rather preclude any interest in an expired bird. Some two or more hours later we returned, pheasant-less, to find three police cars parked in front of the portico.

Cooper opened the door, his smile wan and rather unhappy – evidence that his stoic front was faltering in the face of this latest police invasion.

'Blanket!'

'Certainly, sir.'

Fogg was bundled up and taken off to the kitchens by one of the footmen while the good butler helped me shake the snow off my shooting jacket and took care of hat, scarf and gloves, plus my precious Purdey.

Inspector Swift had been standing beside the Christmas tree observing my entry. He held his notebook and pen and appeared to have been perusing the unopened presents, and I suppose making notes.

He addressed me as I approached. 'Oh, there you are. I was about to send out a search squad.'

'Hardly necessary, Inspector,' I retorted as I sat down to pull off my boots and curse quietly under my breath.

'Would you come upstairs, please, Major Lennox, I have a number of questions I'd like to ask you. I will be in the smoking room.' Swift made his way up with a brisk step as Cooper and I watched him go.

'You'd better distribute those presents, Cooper, looks like Christmas is over.'

'Yes, sir,' he replied with a sigh, 'and the gifts for the Countess, sir?'

'Best return them to their owners,' I told him, being the only reasonable action I could think of.

I took the seat opposite Swift beside the fire. We were both pretty tense, me more than him – which was hardly a surprise given what was at stake. He took up his pen and held it poised on a page, waiting for me to drop my guard.

'Your cousin, Mr Edgar Coleman, has requested we fire your gun in the room where the murder took place, Major Lennox. I have agreed to do this.'

'Big of you,' I replied. 'You must know enough about firearms to realise the shot could not possibly be heard downstairs.'

'Correct. My own thoughts exactly.'

I was somewhat taken aback – the man may have some

merit after all. 'Well,' I stuttered, 'that should cause you to reconsider my guilt.'

'That remains to be resolved,' he replied gravely.

Sergeant Webb put his head around the door. 'Did you 'ear it?'

'Hear what?' I asked.

'The shot! We just fired the pistol. Did you 'ear it, Inspector?'

'No,' Swift replied. 'What about down in the hall? Did any of the men report hearing it?'

'Nope, nothing,' Webb confirmed. 'And I told 'em to keep their ears open.'

'Thank you, Sergeant.' Inspector Swift dismissed him and turned to me. 'Your fingerprints were on the murder weapon.'

He had a habit of firing off statements and questions that took one unawares – it was jolly disconcerting.

'I know. I picked it up when I found her. And even if I hadn't, you would have found my prints on it – it's my gun.'

'Actually –' he leaned back in his seat eyeing me closely '– there was only one set of prints.'

I nodded, though I didn't understand what he was implying.

'I'd have expected to see multiple sets of your prints smeared and smudged from normal use. But there was only one single set, very clear and precise.'

'You mean someone wiped the handle clean prior to my picking it up? Ha! That blows a hole right through your accusations.'

'It's an anomaly.' That was the closest Swift was going to get to agreeing with me.

'No, it's not. It's direct evidence of a set-up.'

'As I said, it's an anomaly.'

Well, this was progress of sorts.

'And the window frame? It's been wiped clean too.'

'How do you know that?' He looked at me sharply.

'Because I checked the drawing room yesterday. And you should have fingerprinted my rooms.' I could switch tangents too, and the accusation took him by surprise. 'I told you at the time, somebody must have been in my rooms and stolen my gun. I even wrote it in my statement, and you still didn't do anything about it.'

He looked perplexed and angry at the same time – no mean feat, but he was on a sticky wicket, and he knew it.

'Very well,' he conceded. 'I agree. We should have fingerprinted your rooms.'

This caused me to sit up in surprise – now here was an honest man prepared to admit to an error.

But he wasn't for quitting, and he returned to his questioning forthwith.

'Tell me why you had a loaded revolver in your possession.'

'Ah …' That gave me pause for a moment. 'Bit of a phobia, actually – since the War.' I ran my fingers through my hair. 'I have trouble sleeping without it. Stupid, I know – and it's just a peashooter. Bloody hard to kill anyone with it, and that's the point, really. It would stop someone, cause some damage, but you'd have to put it to someone's head to kill them.'

'Which is exactly what was done with it,' the Inspector stated.

'Yes.' I nodded, the vision of the Countess's body coming back to mind. 'I was thinking about that. Judging by the proximity and angle of the shot, the murderer must have been close enough to be almost embracing her. Whoever did it must have been on good terms with her.'

'Agreed. But it didn't have to be an embrace,' Swift responded. 'It could have been someone offering to fix something in her hair, or possibly adjusting her necklace.' He looked up from his notebook to stare at me. 'Which appears to have vanished, by the way.'

'I told you at the time it must have been stolen, and I put that in my statement too. The marks on her neck all but confirmed it.' I leaned back in my chair. 'And you and your men can't find it, can you? You searched me and the drawing room very, very thoroughly that night. You know I didn't have it on me, you know it wasn't hidden in the room and you know it wasn't dropped out of the window because your men scoured that area by lamplight. And if I didn't take it, someone else must have done.'

He clamped his lips tightly shut, and I notched another one up to me. Cooper came in just at that moment with a tray laden with coffee pot, cream jug and cups. The Inspector and I shared the refreshments in silence until I broke it.

'The killer couldn't approach the Countess with a gun in hand, it must have been hidden.'

He nodded. 'We found small fibres embedded in the wound; the weapon must have been wrapped in a handkerchief or a scarf when it was fired.'

'You've carried out a post-mortem already?'

'No, but I had a good look at her on the slab this morning. The doctor will be starting on the body after lunch.'

'The shot didn't perforate, did it? There was barely any blood.'

'Correct, there was no exit wound.' He eyed me curiously, holding his head slightly to one side. 'What point are you making?'

'A perforating shot bores a hole from entry to exit point, and there's a risk that it won't be instantly fatal. When a penetrating shot enters the body, it either buries itself in bone, or, more frequently, it bounces around destroying soft tissue. It's far more likely to kill instantly if fired through the temple downward into the brain. It seems the killer knew that – unless it was a fluke, of course, but in the circumstances I'd say that was unlikely.'

'Interesting. You realise you have just made an even stronger case against yourself.'

'Not necessarily. Just about anyone who's been through the War would know that.'

'I went through it,' Swift replied quietly. 'In the trenches, and then a desk job after being gassed. I did not have your expert knowledge of firearms, nor how precisely they need to be applied, until I joined the police force. So I don't agree that it could be just anyone.'

'Anyone brought up to hunt and shoot game has the knowledge.'

'Ah, yes, the landed gentry – perfectly designed for doing nothing at all.'

I took the comment as an insult and glared at him accordingly. Admittedly Edgar very often said much the same, but he did with a disarming charm.

Swift continued: 'I'm not a political person, Major Lennox, so let us concentrate on the murder of this poor lady. What else did you observe?'

I stewed for a moment, then said, 'It was a right-handed shot.'

'Unless the killer was behind her,' Swift countered.

'No, the shot had to be from the front of the skull going down into the brain stem. The angle determines the outcome, and the killer would know it would be virtually impossible from behind.'

'What caused the loud bang?' He had changed the subject again, although by now I was becoming accustomed to his tactics.

'I have no idea.'

'Why was there candle wax in the fire?'

'Oh, you found that too.'

'We did. We took samples for analysis. What do you know of it?'

'No more than you. Maybe the murderer tossed it into the hearth to distract the Countess's attention – in which case it's more likely to be a servant.'

Swift mused on that for a moment. 'Sergeant Webb

interviewed the domestic staff while you were out this morning; there's no doubt that all the servants were together, with the exception of Cooper and the footman, Cartwright, who were both in the hall with the family group. You are the only person without an alibi when the shot went off.' He stared at me keenly, leaning forward to watch my reaction.

'Except we've just established that the shot that was heard down in the hall was not the shot from the pistol, so in fact you don't know when she was killed, do you.'

He opened his eyes at that and sat up. 'You could have staged it,' he countered. 'I think you're more than capable of devising such a strategy.'

'Absolute nonsense. If I had wanted to kill her, why go to the trouble of setting myself up to start with? Your case has a hole a mile wide in it, Swift,' I retorted with satisfaction. Then I stood up abruptly and walked out, leaving him to contemplate his evidence alone.

Ha! I grinned as I strode off down the corridor feeling a good deal more confident in my future. I set off in search of lunch and found the family and the Kingsleys gathered in the dining room.

'Greetings, Uncle, greetings Edgar.' I smiled my best and nodded to the others, including the dreary Gertrude, who stared at me open-mouthed. Natasha was absent, which I have to admit was rather a relief; I wasn't ready for any more histrionics.

'I'm surprised to see you, Lennox,' Sir Peregrine retorted with a supercilious raising of the eyebrows. 'I thought you'd have the decency to spare us your presence until your innocence –' he paused for effect '– or otherwise is proven.'

'The Bill have given me the run of the place, and if you'd care to spare the time to talk to Inspector Swift you might find he doesn't have any firm evidence against anyone – including me,' I retorted tartly.

'You are surely suffering a delusion, Lennox,' Peregrine continued. 'The case against you is virtually impregnable.'

'Yes,' Adam chipped in, 'but I'm here to help, and we'll drag this through every court in the country, old chap. It's going to take months for them to get anywhere. Years even.'

'Shut up will you, Adam,' Edgar snapped. 'Lennox, what did the Inspector say?'

'Yes, about the noise from the gun,' Uncle added. 'Edgar was very determined, you know. He insisted they test it today.'

'And they did.'

I gave them an edited version of what had passed between Swift and myself, over an exceedingly tasty lunch of game pie followed by more plum pudding with custard, accompanied by a brandy snifter. An excellent repast, and I felt very full and content, as if I'd been to all intents and purposes acquitted of the charges pretty much by my own efforts.

The assembled company reacted well to my news, barring Adam of course; but it did thaw the frost, and that was the main thing.

We decamped after lunch to the morning room as none of us could quite face the drawing room, even though the police had given permission for the servants to clean it up. Edgar went off to retrieve Natasha and must have spent considerable time and effort convincing her of my innocence, because he escorted her down to join us about an hour later. She looked pale and weary but came and embraced me warmly.

'I cannot put into adequate words how sorry I am for your loss, dear Natasha,' I told her sincerely.

She looked at me with a pale face and eyes verging on tears.

'Thank you, Lennox. My last living relative is lost to me. If it were not for Edgar and you and dear Uncle Charles, I would be a miserable orphan alone in the world.'

That choked me up somewhat, and I saw Uncle fumble for his handkerchief and take a good sniff. Even Peregrine managed a sympathetic expression.

'Yes, but let's not forget that there's still a murderer in the house!' Adam chipped in, ruining the whole sentiment.

'Will you shut up, Adam,' we all turned and yelled at him.

We passed the next couple of hours in traditional post-Christmas activities, with rounds of cards, followed by a competitive game of Fox and Geese, then a piano recital by Natasha playing Russian folk songs, which was moving and melancholy and heartening all at the same time. We sang Christmas carols after that. Cooper brought in the afternoon tea trolley as dusk fell outside the windows. He was handing out plates of triangular sandwiches and scones when a footman arrived on the scene carrying Mr Fogg in his arms.

'He chased the telegram boy, Your Lordship.' The footman addressed his master, although it was my hound that had perpetrated the crime.

'Put him down, lad, put him down,' Uncle instructed him.

'Apologies,' I said. 'He has a prejudice against postmen and telegram-boys in general.' I did the best I could as Fogg dashed around the room, jumping up and causing people to raise their cups and plates out of reach.

'Who was the telegram for?' Edgar asked.

'Major Lennox, sir. But the Inspector heard the commotion and requested a look at it, and then he kept it, sir.'

'He has no right to do that,' I protested.

'Yes, he has, actually,' Adam said. 'You're still under house arrest, he can do what he likes.'

I turned to tell him to mind his own business when Inspector Swift arrived in the doorway and stood there staring grimly into the room – staring at me, as it happened.

'Major Lennox,' he intoned in that serious voice of his. 'A telegram has just arrived for you from your place of residence. It is from a Doctor Cyril Fletcher.'

All eyes were suddenly riveted upon him.

'Well? What does it say?' I asked, although I could have a damn good guess.

The Inspector held up the yellow telegram card and read it out.

'Lennox. Stop. Your corpse had heart attack. Stop. Too fat. Stop. Police given up investigation. Stop. Got away with it this time, ha, ha. Stop. Who is Countess Sophia? Stop. Yours etc. Cyril Fletcher MD. Stop.'

CHAPTER 10

That put the cat among the pigeons, and all my efforts at redeeming myself seemed to fizzle in a flash. As the assembled multitude sat frozen in shock, I stood up, went toward the Inspector, walked straight past him and headed down the passage.

'Major Lennox,' he called, trying to keep up with me. 'Major Lennox, I must insist on talking to you.'

'Yes,' I snapped. 'And we will do so in the privacy of the smoking room.'

We resumed the seats we had occupied during the interview this morning. I was swearing under my breath – that telegram could have arrived at a better time, or preferably not at all.

Inspector Swift settled himself into his chair while I rang for a footman to bring more fuel for the fire. The coal was duly delivered, followed by Cooper bearing a brandy decanter on a tray with two crystal glasses. He fussed around us and poured a snifter for me. The Inspector declined. (Apparently, the police don't drink on duty – no wonder they're so dull.)

'Ahem.' Swift sought my attention once butler and footman had retreated. He opened his notebook, placed it carefully on his lap and slowly leafed through numerous closely written pages before arriving at a blank one. He stared at it, then examined the ink level in his fountain pen, then directed his attention at me.

'The dead man. Let's start there shall we, Major Lennox?'

I didn't want to start anywhere, I wanted to go home; this was proving the most torturous experience I'd ever encountered.

'Very well, ask away.'

'Who was he?'

'No idea.'

'Surely you don't expect me to believe that?'

'Ask the local police. Chief Inspector Rawlins at my home village of Ashton Steeple. He handled it.'

Swift wrote the name slowly and precisely in his book, then looked back at me. 'Where did he die?'

'On my doorstep. And that's all I know about him. I repeat, ask Rawlins, he took the body away and made whatever enquiries he thought necessary.'

'You disappoint me, Major Lennox. You spent a good deal of my time this morning almost convincing me of your innocence and now this. You knew the Countess, the telegram proves it, but you failed to mention it.'

'I never met her.'

'I don't believe you.'

'I don't care what you believe. I repeat: I never met the woman until I arrived here.'

'But these events –' he pulled out the telegram from between the leaves of his notebook '– these events must have occurred before you came here.'

'Yes, the day before, actually,' I admitted.

'Please explain that.'

Well, that put me on the spot.

'I needed money.' I ran my fingers through my hair, it was getting to be a bad habit, so I fumbled a box of cheroots from my pocket and lit one.

Swift raised his eyebrows in question.

'I'm hopeless with it. Money, I mean. My parents were, too – well, my father; I'm not sure Mother ever really knew what it was. Her family was immensely wealthy – oil, you know; they had so much they never had to handle it, they just asked for stuff and it appeared.' I was babbling again and told myself to slow down. 'You see, Pa just spent it after Ma died, so when I inherited everything it was nothing but debts and the house was mortgaged to the hilt – still is, actually.' I ran out of steam, tried to cudgel my thoughts, felt somewhat helpless. I took a puff on my cheroot, then tossed it into the fire.

'The announcement of the marriage between your uncle and the Countess must have been a terrible shock for you,' Swift stated.

I sat up straight. 'Why?'

He stared at me narrowly. 'Because she was about to take your inheritance. The money that you needed.'

'Nonsense,' I retorted. 'I'd be amazed if there were any money left in Uncle's coffers, this place must cost a fortune to run. Have you any idea how many servants there are in the house? And there are even more outside.'

'Yes, but it would still be yours one day, and you must have felt anger that she was taking it from you?' He sounded a mite exasperated now.

'I felt sad about the history, but not the house – I could never afford to run it. If it does come to me, I'll have the task of selling it. And then it'll be my name that's written in the annals of our family history as the man who lost the family fortune. And it's not my fault, you know, it's not just me. They're all hopeless with money.'

'Major Lennox, will you please stick to the subject. Did you or did you not know the Countess before you encountered her here?'

'No.'

'Then why did the telegram refer to her?'

'Because her name was on the paper.'

'What paper?'

'The one in the fat man's pocket.'

'And he had a heart attack while visiting you?'

'No, he simply turned up dead on the doorstep!' Really the Inspector was going round in circles.

'Right,' he almost shouted, 'let's try again, shall we? Did you know of the Countess or her name in any way whatsoever before you arrived here in this house?'

'Yes. I told you, I needed money.'

'How was she connected to your need for money?'

'Ah.' I supposed that this was where I had to make a clean breast of it, or nearly clean. 'My mother's necklace,' I began. 'It had a large ruby with diamonds around it. Ugly thing, never liked it, but the ruby was from Macedonia, which is rare, or sought-after, something like that.'

'And …' Swift said, waving his hand around.

'And I let it be known that it was for sale. I told you, I needed some money. The Countess's name was put to me as a potential buyer – the only buyer, actually.'

Swift leaned back in his chair; he looked weary – must have had a long day. 'How was this sale set up?'

'Froggy the Hop,' I replied.

'What!' This time he did shout, and he slammed his pen down on his notebook.

'Would you like some tea?' I asked, 'I find it helps keep you alert, although coffee is even better. I could ring for some?'

'No, thank you. Please tell me again – how was the sale set up?'

'I told you. Froggy the Hop set it up. His real name is Frederick Hopper, he was our squadron air-mechanic and go-to man during the War. If we needed anything and couldn't get it officially, we just asked Froggy to jump to it. That's how he got his name, that and being called Hopper of course.'

As Swift wrote this down I noticed his writing was getting untidy. 'And you continued your acquaintance with "Froggy the Hop" after the war.'

'I wouldn't say he was an acquaintance, but he is useful if one needs anything. Seal fur, for instance, for fly-tying

– very difficult to find nowadays, but Froggy can lay his hands on just about anything.'

The Inspector didn't seem interested in fly lures and carried on with the interrogation. 'Was Hopper involved with the sale of the necklace?'

I nodded. 'Yes, I told you he was. I dropped in to see him when I was in London a few weeks ago, showed him the necklace, asked him to find a buyer. He telephoned about a week later and told me that Countess Sophia was interested in buying it.'

'And?'

'I sent it to him, he sold it to her.'

'And?'

'And that was it until the fat man arrived dead on my doorstep. I assumed he was delivering a message from the Countess, but I never got it.'

'Did you ask "Froggy the Hop" if he knew anything about it?'

'Yes, I called him that same evening. He told me he didn't know a thing about it.'

Swift started writing a list in his notebook, holding it away from me so I couldn't see it. Feeling like the school swot, I got up to jab the fire and then wandered around behind him to get a look. He realised what I was doing and hunched over his writing to put a stop to my snooping, so I gave up and sat down again. The story was good, and hopefully he'd discover that most of it was true. As for the rest – well, I needed to keep that under my hat.

Swift asked for the telephone numbers of Froggy the Hop and Chief Inspector Rawlins (which he could have got himself, but I gave them over). Talking to Froggy wouldn't do him any good: he held a distinct antipathy toward the police – they'd be lucky to get his own name out of him, never mind anything more.

Swift said I could go, but lectured me again not to leave the house or grounds. Dispirited I made my way to Uncle's rooms at the front of the house; I knew he would be fretting over the latest turn of events.

'Uncle,' I greeted him on entering his rooms. 'Edgar.' They both turned round to look at me.

'Lennox, I think you need to tell us what's going on.' Edgar looked pretty angry, then held out the silver-framed photograph I'd given to Uncle as a Christmas present.

'Oh, so you spotted the necklace?' I joined them by the fire; poor Uncle was looking bereft.

'Edgar saw it and found my glasses for me,' Uncle said. 'He asked me to take a close look at it. Heathcliff –' his eyes were red-rimmed '– it was your mother's ruby necklace, wasn't it? The one Sophia wore.'

'It was.' I helped myself to a glass of brandy. 'That's why I brought the photograph with me and gave it to you. I didn't know if Sophia would be here or not, but if she were, I wanted her to see it too.'

'Just a minute,' Edgar interrupted, 'you said you'd never met her.'

'I hadn't, but I knew her name because I'd dealt with her through a third party in the recent past.'

'Did you know she was my fiancée?' Uncle asked. 'Before you came here?'

'No, but I'd heard rumours that you had met. I had no inkling that your relationship had progressed to the point of matrimony. Given my own experience with her, I'd actually considered warning you off before you dropped that piece of news on me.'

'I think you need to explain, Lennox – and don't leave anything out,' Edgar demanded.

I told him a more concise version of what I'd told the Inspector, including the fat man's demise and the missing hat. They both looked rather blank when I finished – even I realised it was a strange tale.

'But why did you want Sophia to see the photograph of your mother wearing the ruby necklace?' Uncle asked pointedly.

'Quite,' Edgar exclaimed. 'She'd bought it from your Froggy friend and probably didn't know or care where it came from.'

'Because the Countess paid for it with a bank draft, and when I tried to cash it, it turned out to be a bloody fake. She defrauded me out of a lot of money, and she kept the damn necklace.'

That shocked them, and so it should have – it had been a shock to me at the time.

'Why the devil didn't you say something?' Edgar asked, not unreasonably.

'What was I supposed to say? When I arrived here, the first thing Uncle told me was how happy she'd made him.

I'd never met her, and I have no idea what message the fat man was trying to deliver – maybe it was all a mistake? Maybe he was delivering the money she owed me? That would explain why the driver ran off with the hat.'

'Did you tell the police about this?' Edgar demanded.

'Everything except the fraud, because that just makes my motive for shooting her even more damning.' I needed another snifter and poured a large one.

'I think I'll have one too, Lennox,' Edgar said.

'And I,' Uncle added. 'I feel rather in need of something stronger than sherry.'

We drank together in silence, then Edgar asked, 'So did you discuss the fake bank draft with Sophia at all while you were here?'

'No. Though she did eventually recognise my name. The draft was made out to Major Lennox, but Uncle called me Heathcliff – it was a while before she made the connection. I think she wanted to see me to discuss it. Do you remember her asking? It was after that awful revelation about Uncle's will.'

'God, what a bloody mess.' Edgar sounded dejected.

Uncle looked at us with terrible sadness in his eyes. His fiancée was proving to be a complete mystery; she'd already persuaded him to disinherit us in her favour, God knows what other plans she may have had for him.

And Edgar would have to discover what Natasha knew – if anything. But then what would he do? Tell her that her aunt was a possible fraudster? Or should he try to hide it from her? Or maybe she knew?

Cooper arrived to usher Uncle off to bed, and we bade him good night. Edgar headed off, too, and I ventured to my own rooms, to find Adam lurking in the doorway.

'Been trying to have a word with you all evening, Lennox.'

'The last thing I need is any words with you.'

'Ah, but I have some news, old boy. Thought I'd deliver it in person.'

'What?' I asked crossly. I entered my bedroom; he followed me in like a bad smell.

'The Old Bill are trying to charge bail, but I've managed to evade their ridiculous demands.'

'Why the hell should I give them bail, I haven't done anything. "Innocent until proven guilty" and all that,' I reminded him in exasperation.

'Yes, but that's not quite the way the system works, Lennox. Anyway, you don't need to worry about it, I've fixed it all up.'

'What have you done, you bloody toad?'

'I must protest, old thing, that's hardly the way to talk to your legal man. You're only loose in this house because of me, you'd have been locked up in gaol otherwise.' He sat on the bed, bouncing a little, setting the springs squeaking. Foggy growled from underneath.

I raised my voice. 'If someone hadn't framed me, I wouldn't be in this predicament at all!'

'Good story, Lennox! Repeat that as often as possible.' Adam beamed.

'Tell me about the bail, Adam, and then clear off.'

'They wanted your car, but I told them they couldn't have it. I have placed it outside of their purview.'

'How?'

'I've sequestered it! Put a legal lien on it in lieu of fees owed. Now they can't touch it!' He got to his feet.

'You bounder, Adam!' I yelled as he disappeared out of the door.

CHAPTER 11

Forgot to draw the curtains because I went to bed with my mind troubled and couldn't sleep. When I woke up it was already daylight. I watched large flakes of snow fall slowly in a windless dawn; some landed on the glass, sliding down to join a pile of others on the sill – the weather hadn't improved at all.

My car was now in hock to that toad Adam Kingsley. It was the final straw. *I am not a soft touch. I am not a hapless victim. I am Major Heathcliff Lennox, flyer and soldier, late of the Royal Flying Corps, and I am going to uncover the blighter who has visited these outrages upon me.* I wrote the aforesaid in my notebook and proceeded to jot down a list of questions that I had to find answers to. To my mind, the art of finding answers lies in asking the right questions, and the question first and foremost in my mind was 'What time was the Countess murdered?'

The last time I saw her alive was at the noonday meeting in the dining room on Christmas Eve, when she arbitrarily informed Edgar and myself that she had manoeuvred Uncle into disinheriting us and had sacked Kingsley father and son to boot. That ended shortly before one o'clock in the afternoon and I found her body just a tad after six. Natasha would probably know best what her Aunt had been doing during the missing hours, but there was someone who probably knew the answers without my having to interrogate the poor girl because he had eyes and ears everywhere.

This master of intelligence entered quietly at that moment with my breakfast on a tray.

'Cooper!' I greeted him with a broad smile.

'Ah, good morning, sir, I am gratified to find you in fine spirits.'

'And a very good morning to you! Where's Fogg?'

'I looked in on you earlier, sir, but you were asleep. Mr Fogg chose to accompany me downstairs for a short walk in the garden and breakfast in the kitchen, where he has remained, sir.'

'Excellent!' I clapped my hands and rubbed them together. 'Cooper, I need your help.'

His face took on a guarded look. 'I will do what I can within my limited means, sir.'

He laid breakfast out on my small table beside the fire, which someone had set alight with a merry blaze, and I partook of my favourite meal of the day in dressing gown and slippers.

'No call for alarm, I'm not asking you to dispose of a body.' I laughed. 'Information, Cooper, that's all I want.'

'Sir,' was his terse riposte to that announcement.

'You are in charge of this house, Cooper. You run the whole caboodle, and you know everything that happens.'

His eyes took on a glazed appearance, somewhat like Greggs's did when I asked him to bathe Fogg. 'What were the Countess's movements in the hours before she died, Cooper?' I asked him between mouthfuls of bacon and egg.

'I couldn't say, sir.'

'Yes, you can.' I eyed him sternly, which had no effect so I changed tack. 'Please, Cooper, my neck's on the line here.'

'Very well, sir.' He straightened his back – I imagine there's some sort of butlering code against informing on house guests, and I got the impression he had to steel himself to dish the dirt. 'After Mr Edgar and yourself left for lunch in your car –' his voice wobbled a bit, but he composed himself and continued '– Her Ladyship remained in the dining room for lunch. Miss Natasha joined her, and they left about an hour later.'

'That would be around two o'clock. Then what?' I probed.

'Her Ladyship returned to her rooms and remained there for some time.' Here Cooper ran out of steam again.

'Cooper just tell me, will you, or this will drag out all morning.'

'Very well, sir. She rang the bell from her rooms at half-past four in the afternoon. I sent Cartwright to attend to her as I was rather preoccupied with ensuring that the cold collation for His Lordship's dinner was prepared and ready.'

'You didn't want to see her, did you?'

'I am always at the disposal of His Lordship's guests, sir.'

'Ha! Can't blame you – and most of the servants were busy getting ready for their annual wassail, weren't they?'

'The Staff Christmas Dinner. Yes, they were, sir, but such an event would not prevent them from fulfilling their duties.'

'So what did she want from Cartwright?' I prompted.

'Her Ladyship had formed the habit of taking tea at five o'clock in the drawing room, often with Miss Natasha or His Lordship. As they each have their own preferences, she would usually inform the staff which member of the family was accompanying her. However, on the day in question, she merely requested an additional tray of tea and dainties.'

'So you've no idea who the guest may have been?'

'I do not, sir.'

'Was it someone from the house or someone from outside?'

'We would have to be notified if an outside guest were arriving; as would the lodge-keeper – so it would have been a guest from the house, sir.'

'Does any of your staff know who it was?'

'No, sir, and I have questioned them closely, as have the police.'

Another mystery. I finished my meal and looked at Cooper from my vantage point by the fire: a most superior butler, dutiful, good-hearted and loyal to a fault. I had no reason to doubt his word – unless he did it, of course!

'Was that all she asked for?'

He shifted almost imperceptibly from one foot to the other.

'Umm ...'

'Spit it out, man.'

'Very well, sir. She had prepared a telegram, and requested it be sent immediately.'

'Really?' This made me sit up. 'What did it say?'

'I have not enquired of Cartwright, sir, it would not be discreet. Nor would he volunteer such information to me.'

'Send him up later, would you.' I'd wager Cooper did know what was in that telegram but didn't want to be caught out gossiping. 'Did you tell the Bill about this?'

'They were rather excited about the news of the unknown person who was coming for tea, and they did not think to ask me the question.'

'Excellent, keep it that way if you can, Cooper. What did she do after that?'

'She dismissed Cartwright, telling him she did not desire any member of staff to be present.'

I nodded, taking it all in. 'And there weren't any servants around the house after five o'clock anyway, were there?'

'There was only myself, sir, and Cartwright, who was the footman assisting me that day. We were together all afternoon, first preparing the cold buffet, then the hall for the gift exchange, and then the punch before we took our stations at the gong-ringing. I can confirm that every other member of the indoor staff was seated in the Servants' Hall. Their gift exchange also takes place at six o'clock on Christmas Eve, sir, and nobody was absent from the event.'

'What about the outdoor servants?"

'The police have questioned the head gardener, sir; he confirms that his staff were gathered in the glasshouse for their annual Christmas dinner. They hold exactly the same festival as the indoor staff and at the same hour. It is our tradition, sir.'

'And an excellent one it is too!' I exclaimed.

It's astonishing what can be learned by asking a few questions, I'd never had the faintest idea that all this went on in the house, and it's been my second home all my life.

Cooper had his hand on the doorknob, hoping to escape, when I threw another question at him.

'One other point. My car keys – any idea where they might be?'

'Ah.' He almost allowed a grin to escape. 'Mr Adam has been asking for them, sir.'

'I'll bet he has. What did you tell him?'

'That they are currently mislaid, sir. As are the keys to the coach house in which the car is garaged.'

'Ha! Has he been threatening you with the law?'

'He did mention something of the kind, sir, but it did not seem to make the keys any easier to locate.'

Cooper withdrew before I could extend my interrogation, but I was happy enough with the outcome, the securing of my Bentley – good old Cooper! I recall how Adam used to play practical jokes on him when we were youngsters; the old fellow would have enjoyed finding a way to thwart Adam's latest bit of skulduggery.

I bathed, togged up in warm tweeds and jacket and went off in search of my dog and a long walk. But the proposed expedition came to nought: Fogg refused to leave the warmth of the kitchen, and when I set foot across the threshold to the outside world I discovered why. The snow was now knee-deep and still falling in fat flakes – it was quite beautiful. The branches of the trees along the entire length of the drive were covered in soft white layers. The ground was virgin all the way down to the gates in the walls, and the pretty little lodge next to it looked like an iced confection from a fairy tale. I let out a long breath – well, at least we wouldn't be infested by the Old Bill today, a cart horse wouldn't get through that lot, never mind a modern motor car.

I knew most of the rest of the house to be idle lay-a-beds, so I returned to my rooms to regroup. Cooper had diligently delivered the unopened Christmas gifts as requested and mine were still sitting in a stack on a coffer in my bedroom. I tucked them under my arm and headed off to wake Edgar up so we could unwrap them together.

He didn't seem too keen on the idea.

'Lennox, what the devil do you mean by charging in here at this hour? It's barely daylight.'

'We're having a belated Christmas, I've brought my

presents to open.' I tossed them into a chair by his blazing fire – one of the servants must have been in to light it while he was asleep. 'Where are yours?' I scanned the room but couldn't see any sign of them.

Edgar tugged at the bell pull for someone to fetch his breakfast. 'We did it already. Natasha and I opened our gifts yesterday while you were helping the police with their enquiries.'

That knocked me back a bit – it was a reminder that he had Natasha now, and our relationship was changed.

'Very well. I'll go and see if Uncle's awake.' I gathered up the offerings under my arm.

'Don't!' He put his hand up to halt me. 'Uncle opened his with us at the same time.'

I must have looked slightly crestfallen, as he added, 'For heaven's sake, Lennox, give me a couple and we'll open them together.'

Grinning, I sat down on the edge of his bed and threw him the two gifts from the Kingsleys, and we ripped the paper off, balling it up and throwing it at each other just as we'd done since we were small boys. He held up a scarf and tie-pin from the lawyers; I unwrapped a pair of woollen socks from Natasha. Gertrude's offering was a tortoiseshell comb, which I hoped wasn't stolen as it was actually rather nice. Uncle had gifted me a very smart quilted dressing gown to replace my old tattered one.

Edgar had bought me a nifty pocket torch which very much took my fancy, having never owned one of these new-fangled 'flashlights'.

'Ha! Thanks, old man, I've rather been hankering after one of these.' I switched it on and off, and then he grabbed it from me.

'No, like this!' Edgar showed me how to change the strength of the beam and I marvelled at it for a moment – amazing how far we have developed modern technology, from candles to gas lamps to electricity, and now bat-tery-powered light!

There remained only one present unopened, a long narrow box wrapped with sludge-coloured brown paper and string.

'Who's that from?' Edgar asked.

'Haven't a clue!' I turned it over, searching for a name, but found only my own. 'For Major Heathcliff Lennox' was inscribed neatly on the label tied to the ribbon with brown string. 'The Countess, maybe?'

'Possibly, though the ones we received from her were wrapped in gaudy paper; yours looks very different,' Edgar said.

'How did she give you anything?' I continued looking at the unwrapped box as I asked him. 'I mean, she never made it to the tree that night, did she?

'Natasha found the gifts piled up in her rooms, so she handed them out. I received a red silk tie. Each of us men got the same, including Uncle. I think he was rather upset about it.'

'I'm not surprised: he'd just handed over a ring with a huge diamond set in it, plus the keys to this house, and all he got was a tie. Hardly special, was it?'

'What did she give you?' Edgar asked.

'Nothing, by the looks of it.'

'Strange.' Edgar was watching as I turned the gift over in my hands. 'Lennox, are you going to open that damn box or sit there staring at it?' he asked in exasperation.

I eyed him, grinned and ripped the string and wrapping off. Inside was another box, made from thicker cardboard, and inside that was something wrapped in fine white paper. I laid it on Edgar's bed quilt and unrolled it carefully pulling back layers of delicate tissue paper until I revealed the contents. We both stared – it was my mother's ruby and diamond necklace.

CHAPTER 12

'Well, that beats a tie!' Edgar exclaimed.

I was almost speechless – that blasted necklace had been the cause of so much trouble it was the last thing I wanted to see again.

'Who the devil did this?' I shouted.

Edgar picked up the wrappings and scrutinised them. 'Can't see a thing on the paper other than your name. Bit late for fingerprinting, too,' he added, laying them aside and picked up the necklace, turning it over in his hands, studying it closely.

'Oh God, Swift will have me in gaol for this,' I groaned.

'Nonsense!' Edgar retorted. 'Why on earth should he?'

'Because it is such an obvious ploy, isn't it? I pretend to receive the necklace as a gift so I can lay a legitimate claim to it. If I'd truly murdered the Countess and stolen it from around her neck how else would I ever be able to bring it to light?'

Edgar thought about it, then remarked, 'And the killer brings the finger back around to point at you again.' He suddenly looked up at me. 'Someone really has it in for you, old boy.'

At that moment a knock sounded on the door, and Cooper entered with Edgar's breakfast tray, but stopped suddenly in his tracks. 'Isn't that …' he stuttered.

'Yes, damn it!' I swore, then got up, shoved the thing in my pocket and stalked out.

I didn't get very far because Edgar came bounding after me. 'Lennox, come back right now.'

'Edgar, this is driving me to insanity. I need to think.' I carried on walking.

'Then I'll think along with you. But come back, have some toast and jam and we'll work something out between us.'

We returned to his room, Cooper set up the tray by the fire, and we both sat down and nibbled on the delicious food. I didn't have much since I'd already eaten, but it made me feel a little better.

'I'll have to tell the police.'

'Yes, of course,' Edgar said. 'Are they here?'

'No, the snowfall is too heavy to allow anyone to come or go.'

'So you have at least one day to make some progress. I suggest you make the most of it.' He took a sip of his favourite Earl Grey tea. 'And I'll help all I can.'

'Thanks,' I said. 'And Edgar …'

'Yes?'

'Did you do it?'

The tea almost exploded from his mouth. He managed to swallow it before bursting into laughter.

'What the devil is so funny? I've been dreading asking you that.'

He wiped his mouth on a clean napkin and answered, 'The fact that you've finally matured enough to ask difficult questions instead of ducking them, Lennox. Welcome to the real world!'

'Oh, very amusing, Edgar.'

'But no, I did not kill her. Though I can't say I'm going to mourn the woman, because I'm not.'

I went on my way – I had the remainder of the day to work out who might be the real murderer; a murderer who was devilish tricky and seemed to be miles ahead of my own fumbling efforts. Can't say that I'm a God-botherer, but I did send Him a short prayer for a lot more snow.

Cartwright was a talkative man. In fact it was very difficult to get him to shut up long enough to answer anything at all. I had removed the small table and requested that Cooper set up a proper desk in my bedroom, next to the fire. It had taken some time and quite a bit of furniture rearranging, but I had a proper HQ from which to work. I started by prioritising the list of tasks in my notebook, and Cartwright was at the top of it, which was why he now stood in front of me.

'Tell me again, in just a few words, what happened when you told the Countess that the telegraph office was already closed for the festive holiday.'

'Ah, well, sir. It's like I says already. She'd called me to her rooms. And she'd written these words down on some paper she had, but it didn't make no sense. The best I could make of it was: "Porkie. Where you are? Has to tell me. He is here. Him." So I says all over again that it will "have to wait on account of the holiday – it being after midday on Christmas Eve and the exchange will already be shut down". But she kept telling me I have to make them open it. Well, this is England, ain't it? We might look after the gents and ladies like, but even royalty can't order the telegraph office around.'

'Yes, yes, thank you, Cartwright.' I held my hand up to stop the flow. 'And you don't know who it was meant for? The telegram, I mean.'

'No, on account of it was burned. She had it all ready for me. I asked her how many words 'cause the cost is by the number of words, but then she started on about how urgent it were. She kept on saying she would pay more for it to go straight off, but I said it don't matter how much she paid, 'cause it wasn't going nowhere. Then she shouted and screwed up the paper and threw it at me! It bounced straight off me head and into the fire, so it did. It weren't right to throw it at me. I told Cook about it and Mr Cooper, but he was in trouble hisself with the lady so there weren't much he could do.'

'Good, good. No, I mean I'm sorry to hear she treated you so badly, Cartwright. Um, did you see anyone at all in her rooms, or anyone in the drawing room when you took the tea tray up later at five o'clock?'

'No, and it was five minutes before five, on account of our Christmas Dinner. There were only her in the room, no one else, and she were all dressed up already. She had all her jewels on, glittering they was, never seen no one wearing so many rings in my life, and that raspberry stone all set with diamonds was round her neck, and she had the dangling watch thing, too. Foreign that was, mark you, and old – only thing she wore as was old. Didn't glitter like the others.'

That was it! Good Lord, that was it. I knew something was missing – it was the small watch she always wore, like something a nurse would wear; she kept it pinned among the frills of her dress. I almost shook the man's hand, I was so pleased.

'Thank you, Cartwright.' I told him. 'Well done, man!'

He looked askance at me, probably not quite understanding why I was so excited, but he departed happily enough.

Gertrude took the watch from the body! I was sure of it and lost no time in noting this down in my book before going off to find her – time really was of the essence.

No one answered my knock on the door of the Italian suite, so I sought her in the breakfast room, where I found Peregrine Kingsley reading a newspaper over a leisurely plate of kippers.

'Nothing today,' he drawled.

'What?'

'Yesterday's paper. This.' He shook his newspaper at me. 'It's from yesterday. No one could deliver today's. Hopeless. Always the same in this rural backwater.'

I was about to snap back that he didn't have to come

to this 'rural backwater', but decided I had bigger fish to fry.

'Have you seen Gertrude?'

'No, I have not. Why do you ask? Are you going to shoot her too?"

'No, not her, nor anyone – I don't shoot people.' That really riled me, but I kept my head and sat down in my usual place at one end of the table. 'I overheard your conversation with Natasha in the smoking room. Were you having an affair, and the Countess forbade it? Maybe you shot her.'

His reaction surprised me. He turned deathly pale and stared at me in utter astonishment, deflating before my eyes. 'I-I-I ...' he stuttered. 'No, no. It's over. She cast me aside.' He pulled himself together but was still very shaken – I'd hit a very raw nerve and decided to press the advantage.

'Did the Countess force her to give you up?'

He suddenly straightened up, ran a hand down his lapel and looked at me, his usual arrogant poise almost resumed intact. 'I am not going to discuss this with you, Lennox. It is none of your business.' Kingsley rose to leave, his breakfast unfinished on his plate.

'Talk to me or the police, take your pick,' I told him.

'You'll tell them anyway.'

'That depends. I'm willing to keep confidences, but not vital evidence. If I tell the police, you'll have to spill it, and Natasha will be questioned too. And Edgar and Uncle will get to hear of it, so take your pick.'

He sat down again and stared at his hands. 'We were –' he stuttered, then got a grip '– we were very close. I had hopes ... I thought we might even wed one day. But then she cooled off, lost interest in me. I suppose the age difference became too great for her, I don't know.' His voice trailed off again.

'When did you meet?' I asked.

'Earlier this year, when she and the Countess arrived in London. I knew some of the Russian nobles who were already in London, and we met at a ball given by one of the royal families, cousins to the Tzar himself. She took my breath away, such a dazzling creature. I would do anything for her. Anything.'

This was a new experience for me. Feeling sympathy for Peregrine Kingsley – who'd have thought it.

'Did your liaison end before or after she met Edgar?'

'Before, he had nothing to do with it.'

'Do you know that they're engaged to be married?'

He put his head in his hands and nodded. 'She told me that night. The night you overheard us.'

'Was the Countess responsible for ending your love affair?' I asked again.

'No. No,' he replied emphatically.

'Where were you between five o'clock and six o'clock on the evening the Countess was shot?'

'You're trying to trap me, Lennox. Don't play games with me. I was nowhere near that damn woman that night. Ask Adam, I was with him and Gertrude until we went down to the hall for the gift-giving.'

'That is not correct.'

At these words, we both swivelled around. Gertrude was standing in the doorway and regarding us with that expressionless face she has. She was clutching her large handbag, a pose reminiscent of a praying mantis; then she walked rapidly into the room and slid into a chair, staring intently at Kingsley all the while.

'I was. Do not contradict me on the matter, Gertrude. Adam will confirm my presence.' He leaned toward her in a bullying manner. I opened my mouth to remonstrate, but she remained cool and unconcerned.

'No, Peregrine, you were not with us in our rooms at those times; and Adam was not there either. It was only I.' She spoke in a strange, almost mechanical manner, and I realised that she'd been taught to speak by an elocution specialist – which may have helped her pronunciation but had resulted in a voice devoid of all inflection and emotion.

Kingsley looked from me to her, then got up and stormed from the room. Can't say I was sorry to see him go – and he had now moved up my list to suspect number one. At this rate I'll have it cracked before the police have even got out of bed!

'Gertrude.' I wasn't sure how to start a delicate conversation with someone who was so very odd. 'May I ask you a question?'

'You may.' She stared intently back at me, clutching the handles of her handbag on her lap.

'Do you have in your possession a small watch belonging to the Countess?'

'I do.'

'May I see it please?'

'Yes,' she said but didn't move.

I waited, nothing happened. 'Now?'

'Yes.' She unclasped her bag and rummaged through it, holding it away from me so I couldn't see inside it; then she drew something out. She slid her hand across the table and opened her fingers to reveal the small watch, which was now a brightly polished silver colour.

I looked at it, unsure what to do next. The hands were showing an incorrect hour: it was currently just after nine thirty in the morning, but the watch was showing eight twenty. My heart sank a little as I was hoping it might have stopped at the moment the Countess was shot.

'Do you recall what time you found the watch on the body of the Countess?'

'I do,' Gertrude answered.

'And what was it?'

'It was four minutes past six in the evening.'

'Very good. What time was showing on the Countess's watch?'

'It showed five forty-five.'

'Really? Marvellous. That must have been the moment she was killed – and it was the same time as the gong was sounded. That makes perfect sense: it was before we all went downstairs, not afterwards.' I was thrilled – I'd uncovered the answer I was searching for; but then I realised it didn't quite add up. 'Why is it showing a different hour now?'

'Because I have wound it up.'

'Why?'

'Should I address you as Lennox, or Heathcliff, or Major Lennox?'

'Lennox, please.'

'Very well, Lennox. You may call me Gertrude.'

'I already did.'

'But we were not introduced. It has been very difficult to converse with you as we were not correctly introduced.'

'Ah, yes, I remember, I came to greet you. I do apologise.' Good heavens, somebody had really drummed the formalities into this girl.

'I realise you may think it unusual that I acquire items from around the house.'

'Yes, and people's pockets – like my Montblanc pen?'

She gave me a cold stare. 'Correct. I do so because these items are poorly treated. They are in need of attention, and so I gather them and clean them and, if necessary, repair them.

'Hum.' I recall that my pen had been returned not only polished but with ink in it; plus, it was working, which it hadn't done in a long time. 'Is that why you take things? To put them in order.'

'Correct. I feel uncomfortable in a disorderly environment.'

'May I pick up the watch, please?'

'You may.' Gertrude inclined her head.

I reached over and scrutinised it in the palm of my hand. Now I knew why detectives use magnifying glasses: the face was very small and plain, although it did have something written on it in Russian Cyrillic lettering. I turned it over, noting that there was no engraving on the metal, which was not, in fact, silver but something more like tin. Nor was it originally designed to be worn on the breast: it had been a wristwatch, and the missing strap had been replaced by a bent safety-pin. I put it to my ear and heard a distinct tick. It was working. But when I placed it back on the table, it stopped.

'It's defective, isn't it?'

'Correct,' Gertrude answered. 'The mechanism works when the watch is upright, but if it is placed flat on a horizontal plane, it stops. I have found it impossible to remedy the fault.'

'Which is why it showed the time when the Countess died, because she fell flat on the floor,' I observed, 'and it was probably why she wore it pinned to her chest.'

Gertrude merely nodded, and I assumed she must have got tired of continually saying 'Correct'.

'Gertrude, would you be willing to swear in a statement to the police about all this?'

'Yes, I would.'

'You're not concerned that they might think your habit of – umm – taking and repairing items a touch odd?'

'No, because it is not odd, it is logical. And I tell the truth at all times. The Good Lord is watching each and every one of us; I would be forever condemned to the burning fires of Hell if I told an untruth.'

'Ah yes, quite right,' I muttered in reply. And since she was a compulsive truth-teller, it struck me as a good chance to discover more.

'Do you know where either Peregrine or Adam was when the gong was sounded?'

'No.'

'Did you hear anything around that time?'

'No.'

'Did you see anyone?'

'No.'

'Do you know who shot the Countess?'

'Yes.'

'Who?'

'You.'

This wasn't going well.

Gertrude rose to her feet. 'I am leaving now.'

'Erm, fine, excellent. Can I keep the watch?'

'You may, yes. Good day, Lennox.'

'And to you, too, Gertrude.'

She walked out still clutching her bag, even more mantis-like than on entry. I examined the Countess's watch again, picking it up and setting it down, checking that it did indeed respond as Gertrude had observed. Then I set off for my rooms and notebook, buoyed by the fact I was holding in my hand the very answer I'd been seeking.

CHAPTER 13

I deviated from my course in search of coffee in the kitchens and my dog, who greeted me enthusiastically but was still reluctant to leave the warmth of the stove. Armed with a large cup of steaming brew and a couple of biscuits in my pocket, I headed back to HQ. In my notebook against the question mark about the time of death, I wrote the words *five forty-five p.m.*

So the killer had struck as the gong was being sounded and then calmly came downstairs to join us – or had they? No, they hadn't, because someone had let Mr Fogg out of my rooms and stolen my pistol. Wait. They must have taken the pistol earlier in the day because the Countess was shot on the sound of the gong and I was still in my rooms then and had been for a good hour or more.

I had seen the gun that morning when I opened the drawer searching for my book mark – it could have been taken any time after that. My mind suddenly started racing around in a frenzy of questions, so I made myself sit down and write proper notes just as Inspector Swift did when he was detecting. Next to the question 'What time was the pistol stolen?', I placed a large question mark.

The hour of Fogg's liberation was easier to determine – after five forty-five and before six o'clock. Assuming the killer wasn't in cahoots with anyone, they would have shot the Countess as the gong sounded, rushed up here to my rooms, let the dog loose, and then dashed back to wherever they came from. Then they would have descended the main staircase to join everyone in the hall before six o'clock, armed now only with their gifts. And all this would have had to be done without being seen by a soul.

The servants' staircase was the only answer. The murderer would have used it safe in the knowledge that all the servants were elsewhere. Plus the back stairs were fitted with doors, making them easy to hide behind and close off. This would be how they forced Fogg to take the main passageways, through which he'd soon come searching for me.

I must say I was beginning to form a degree of respect for the blighter because the whole plan seemed very intelligent (on which point alone I questioned the likelihood of Peregrine Kingsley being the murderer). However, he remained top of my list, with Uncle at the bottom and Edgar just above him, and then Cooper because he'd been ringing the gong. I now placed Gertrude above Cooper, because having had quite a long talk with her, I didn't think she seemed the type.

Coffee and biscuits finished, I set off for a jaunt up and down the back stairs, where I encountered Cooper coming up.

'Greetings, Cooper,' I said gaily, 'can't stop, I'm timing myself.'

'Yes, sir. Good day, sir,' he replied, stepping smartly out of my way.

'I am following in the footsteps of a masterly murderer.'

I raced down, stopwatch in hand, and made it from the top of the stairs just outside my bedroom door to the stairs nearest the landing within one minute thirty. Then I turned around and raced back up again, and added up the total, which came to four minutes more or less, plus thirty seconds for letting Fogg out and possibly tossing him a biscuit or two for being a good doggie. I wrote all these details down neatly in my notebook, feeling quite pleased with my efforts.

On the night of the murder, Uncle was already in the hall when I came down, making me the first guest to arrive. Peregrine Kingsley was the last, and he also mentioned my dog, presumably in an attempt to lure me up to the drawing room, where he'd set me up to be caught red-handed. It was all falling into place now; by morning I would have him uncovered, complete with evidence to hand over to the Old Bill when they managed to make it through the snow.

I waltzed off to find Edgar and inform him of my success. He was in the drawing room, book in hand, feet up by the fire and a cigar on an ashtray at his elbow.

'You here, Edgar?'

'Indeed I am. Thought it time we brought this room back into the fold, as it were. Can't keep avoiding it – used to be the most popular place in the house.'

'Yes,' I concurred, ringing the bell for service as I spoke, then sat down opposite in my favoured wing chair by the brightly blazing fire. 'It needs a bit of exorcising. I'll have a brandy to see off the ghost of ladies passed.'

'Good idea.' Edgar closed his book and tossed his cigar into the flames. 'So, what progress?'

As I opened my mouth to tell him, I realised he'd have to hear about Natasha and Peregrine, so I stuttered to a halt. Fortunately, Cooper came in and served us with a small brandy snifter each and enquired if we would like to take lunch in the room. We agreed!

This put off the spilling of the beans until we were sitting either side of the circular card table with a heaped plate of cheesy Welsh rarebit each and a stack of home-baked bread fresh from the oven. I told the whole tale to Edgar as the snow continued to come down outside the window and a whistling wind rattled the panes – a fine contrast to our snug roost indoors.

He took it well, I have to say; in fact, he didn't bat an eyelid.

'Did you know about the romance?' I asked.

'I'd guessed. There was a rather strained atmosphere between them at times and I'd caught his unguarded expression now and then. He appeared almost heart-broken. I discussed it with 'Tasha, which was rather uncomfortable, but it had to be done. Clear the air and all that.'

'I hope this hasn't changed your opinion of Natasha?'

'Not in the slightest, why should it? They parted some time ago, there was nobody in her life when we met and nothing has led me to alter that assumption.'

'And you agree that Peregrine did it?'

'Not at all!' He laughed. 'You're supposed to accuse the culprit based on evidence, not prejudice. I don't like him any more than you do, but anyone could have gone to your rooms, let the dog out and made it back down to the hall in time – including me.'

'Nonsense! It's obviously Peregrine, he had a damn good motive for shooting the Countess.'

'Almost everyone had a motive for shooting her, my dear Lennox. You and I were about to be disinherited. She sacked both Kingsleys, Cooper was about to be tossed out on his ear, Gertrude is potty and the Countess was an embarrassment to Natasha. You need proper evidence.'

'Peregrine lied about where he was when the murder took place.'

'That means he has something to hide, not that he killed anyone.'

I paused to think about this. Edgar was right: the police gathered evidence, I'd seen them do it, they put it in jam jars. Maybe I'd better get some?

As I pondered he continued to raise doubts. 'And why let Fogg out at all? I understand the murderer wanted to lure you to the drawing room but how could they be sure the dog would come downstairs?'

'He was locked out of my rooms and the servants' staircase. He wouldn't just hang around an empty corridor. Maybe they tossed a few biscuits as a trail, but if they knew Fogg they'd know he would come looking for me after a while, and once he found me I would be compelled to take him back up to my rooms. In fact, given the location of my present quarters at the rear of the house, I'm the only person who would go past the drawing room because everyone else is at the front.'

'While we were all together down in the hall,' Edgar mused. 'Yes, very plausible ... there's some risk in the timing, but it could work.'

'It did work!' I exclaimed. 'I'm still suspect number one in the eyes of the police.'

'The loud bang that alerted us in the hall,' he went on, 'that's the key to this. What caused it, Lennox?'

'I have no idea. I think it came from the fireplace, but it went off before I entered. The police found wax in the grate, they believe someone either threw a candle in to divert the Countess's attention, or one fell in somehow.'

'Is it possible that she was holding one in her hand? A Russian Christmas ritual or some such?'

'Perhaps, but she wasn't close enough to have dropped it into the fire when she keeled over; and anyway it was paraffin wax, not beeswax.'

'How do you know that?' Edgar asked.

'I examined it the day after the shooting, took a look

under the grate. Haven't really thought about it until now. Paraffin wax is white and remains white even after it has melted and set again. Beeswax is honey-coloured but turns brown or black when overheated, particularly in a fire.'

'Ah yes, well done. Where was it from, I wonder?'

'Precisely the question I have. We don't have paraffin candles in this house – horrible stuff. We produce our own wax for our own candles from beehives in the grounds. It's very interesting actually – bees, you know: quite fascinating. I keep some in the orchard at the Manor.'

'Ha! Maybe your country ways will come in useful after all. You'd better get detecting and find out where the wax came from. And by the way, Uncle would like to see you this afternoon. He's a bit agitated.'

'About what?'

'The estate – things are a mess. You're the heir, he won't discuss details with me, but you'll need to know.'

'Oh hell.' I ran my fingers through my hair. 'I'll go and see him, but it really is the blind leading the blind on that subject.'

'And on many others.' Edgar laughed.

Poor old Uncle Charles, I found him in his rooms in nightwear despite the hour. We sat at the round reading table, which was now piled with our old family papers and leafed through them. We fretted over events: the loss of his love, the changing of the will, the unchanging of the will, and the terrible state of the estate thanks to bloody Kingsley. I told him my suspicions about Peregrine and he agreed to find a new estate manager, although I knew he wouldn't. We didn't achieve a damn thing. Cooper came in eventually and persuaded him to go and lie down, so I took myself back to my rooms and my personal murder enquiry.

'*Bang?*' I noted down, and then '*Wax?*'

All evidence was gone. After the police had given permission for the drawing room to be brought into use again, Cooper had supervised a thorough cleaning. I had seen Sergeant Webb take away scrapings from the wax left in the grate so the police may have discovered a clue worth following, but it didn't help me.

I remembered a smell, though ... It had vanished pretty quickly thanks to the open window, but I recalled it now. At the time, the shock of finding the body and all the subsequent ballyhoo had pushed it to the back of my mind. It wasn't paraffin wax because that doesn't have an odour; no, it was something more like gunpowder ... And then I realised – flash powder! That's what had caused the noise – a firecracker! We had boxes of them ready for New Year's Eve. They were kept in the gunroom (the house gunroom, not my closet – I don't approve of mixing people's guns, you never know who might get hold of them).

Firecrackers have short fuses. Someone must have wrought a delay on the one that went off in the fireplace because the bang wasn't heard until almost fifteen minutes after the Countess was shot. Modifying it wouldn't have been difficult for anyone who'd ever concocted home-made fireworks. Take a stick, tie a firecracker to it, melt some paraffin wax in a pan over the hearth, dip it like a toffee apple to the thickness desired, and there you have it – a delayed-action firecracker. It would burst with a resounding boom sometime after being popped in a fire. And if it were placed on a log jammed vertically rather than sideways, the delay could be extended – and they were, because I remembered that the logs were a disorderly mess in the grate when I found the Countess. Detecting requires a considerable amount of observation – I read about it in Sherlock Holmes and it is true.

The dinner gong sounded and my investigations ceased for a hearty meal. I must say I was ready for it after a day of strenuous intellectual pursuits.

We ate in the dining room, the first time we'd all sat there together since the night Uncle made the formal announcement of his engagement. It was strange and strained. We took our customary seats; I was with the girls at the end of the table; Natasha was very quiet and didn't seem to want to talk to me, while Gertrude kept eyeing the silver.

'Is there anything you think needs an extra polish?' I asked her.

She was sitting as usual with her bag clasped on her lap. Now she raised a hand slowly and pointed a long thin finger at the salt cellar. I reached over to grab it and turned to a footman standing against the wall. It was Cartwright.

'Would you take this to the silver polisher, please, Cartwright, it needs buffing up.'

'I'll do that, sir, and don't you worry, it won't take a jiffy. He's a good man is Wilberforce, he polishes the silver to a mirror, but he has a bit of a problem you see. That's why he misses a bit now and then. He's a keen fiddler and he fiddles away till his fingers gets all sore –'

'Cartwright will you just take it. Please!' I shoved it into his hands as Uncle staggered to his feet and banged a spoon on the table.

He led us in prayer in memory of his expired betrothed, and then another for all who were no longer with us. Then there was something else, but my mind rather drifted off until the soup arrived.

I was just tucking in when Natasha turned to me.

'That was a kindness, Lennox, it will help Gertrude. It was clever of you.'

Praise indeed! I opened my mouth to respond, but she now turned to Gertrude.

'Did you see what he did? He had it taken away to be cleaned. Wasn't that kind of him?'

My soup was getting cold amid all this praising, and I was hungry.

'He is like Adam!' Gertrude suddenly exclaimed.

I looked at her – this was serious defamation of character. 'Nonsense, I'm nothing like Adam. Not remotely.'

'Yes! You are Good. The veil has lifted from mine eyes. The Lord made you so, like Adam, even his chosen name marked out his destiny. He is a saint!'

She'd gone all starry-eyed and was gazing from me to him and back – pretty much convinced me she really was completely bonkers.

'Now come along, old thing.' Adam stood up and approached his wife.

'But Adam, I have done wrong among good people, I must confess my deeds. I must atone.'

The assembled were now sitting open-mouthed at the dinner table drama, soup entirely forgotten. Even the servants had halted mid-serve.

'It was only a salt cellar, Gertrude, no need to worry about the other stuff, it was all returned to wherever it came from.' He tried to reassure her – he even put his arm around her thin shoulders.

'Yes, we don't mind at all,' Natasha said in support.

'Apart from my letter-opener – no one's returned that yet,' Peregrine grumbled, but everyone ignored him.

'But I have sinned. You don't understand, Adam. It was I. The Countess. It was I who killed her.'

CHAPTER 14

Well, that caused the collective jaw to drop, as you can imagine; and to think I'd spent days trying to uncover the culprit, not to mention some very uncomfortable hours with the Old Bill – why the devil didn't she say so earlier.

'How could you do such a thing, Gertrude!' Natasha cried out.

'And why?' I asked, which seemed the more to the point.

'She slighted Adam with a cruel snap of her fingers,' Gertrude declared with words of passion, yet still in her deadpan tone. 'She dismissed him like an old sock. He has dedicated his life to caring for people, helping them in their hour of need, and she simply cast him away.'

'You are talking about Adam, aren't you?' Edgar asked, having the same difficulty as the rest of us in recognising the description.

Gertrude turned with suppressed fury toward Edgar. 'Yes. He is a saint! Do you deny him?'

'Gertrude,' Adam said firmly.

She turned to raise her eyes to his, suddenly submissive. 'Yes, husband?'

'You did not kill her,' he told her sternly.

'I did, I did. It was unintended, but I am responsible.' She clutched her handbag closer to her skinny chest.

'Just a minute,' I interjected, 'you can't unintentionally shoot someone in the head. It's just not possible.'

'I used the power of prayer!'

'No, no. Really, old thing, mentioning something in a prayer doesn't necessarily make it come true, you know. If it did we'd all be dropping like flies,' Adam reasoned with her. 'Now, how about we go to our rooms and look at the angels. You could say another prayer to them. Tell them you didn't mean it. Would you like to do that?'

She hesitated, and he took her hand in his. 'Come,' he told her.

'Yes, husband.' She nodded meekly and he led her off. As they exited the room, I caught a glance from Peregrine; it bore a look of hostile intent.

'She will have to go. I've said it before and I'll say it again, she's unhinged. Bedlam's the place, we have no choice left to us.' Peregrine broke the ice with a sledgehammer.

'That is an appalling comment to make.' Natasha turned on him. 'How could you ever consider condemning the poor woman? You really are a snake, Peregrine!' She threw her napkin onto the table and ran out.

Edgar rose to his feet. 'You heartless worm, now look what you've done!' Then he threw his napkin onto the table and left the room in the footsteps of his affianced.

'Absolute nonsense! What is the matter with people? I

was simply stating the truth. Gertrude is beyond eccentric and needs proper attention.' He too threw his napkin onto the table. 'I am retiring to my rooms. Goodnight!'

Well, I threw my napkin onto the table too, it being so damn popular.

'I'm really quite hungry, Uncle,' I said. I got to my feet and went to sit next to him. He was twisting around in his chair to watch his last guest stalk off. 'Shall we skip the soup and order the main?'

'I think we should, Heathcliff.' He looked at me with bemusement in his old eyes. Poor chap, he'd aged more in the last few days than he had in the past decade.

'Cooper, can we start again, please?' I requested of the good fellow.

'Certainly, sir.'

The plates were cleared and the table re-laid for just we two.

'I don't think she's mad, do you?' he asked me with a shake of the head.

'No,' I replied, patting his hand. 'And she didn't murder anyone either. She's just rather sensitive.'

'And special.'

'Yes, special is a good word,' I agreed, as a plate of venison pie, mashed potato, gravy, carrots and beans was placed before me.

Drama gives the appetite an edge, I've always thought, and we enjoyed an excellent repast with copious servings of red wine.

'Heathcliff, do you recall our Christmases when your

Aunt Mary was alive?' Uncle asked with a merry wave of the wineglass as we arrived at the cheese course.

'I do, Uncle. Which one were you thinking of?'

We spent a most pleasant evening talking of the old days and the old folk. I didn't even remind him not to call me Heathcliff. Cooper helped him totter off to bed after finishing the port and a brandy digestif, as I made my way upstairs under my own steam and fell into bed for a deep and restful slumber.

It had stopped snowing. First thing that struck me on awakening to beautiful bright sunshine streaming through my windows – that, and a terrible headache.

'Good morning, sir.' Cooper was at my bedside with a hearty tray of breakfast. Fogg was there too, wagging his bottom, snow on his nose, chocolate brown eyes shining with excitement.

'I feel in need of some powders, Cooper,' I told him, rubbing my forehead.

'You will find them on your tray, sir,' the excellent man replied, and set it on the desk beside the fire, already lit and merrily burning. 'I fear a thaw has begun, sir.'

'Oh, hell. Harbingering the return of the Old Bill, I suppose.'

'Probably not today, sir. But almost certainly tomorrow.'

'Ah, well, I'd better get a move on then, hadn't I?'

I shared my delicious breakfast with Fogg and despite the little matter of a murder to resolve I couldn't resist a tramp through the silent, snow-bound woods with soft sunshine filtering between the trees and my dog at my heels.

Adam was stalking the hall on my return, which caused some disruption to Fogg's blanket routine. Once the hound was bundled up and carried off to the kitchen stove, I turned my attention to the oily toad.

'How's Gertrude today?'

'Better. Mostly better.' He seemed less emollient, as though the wind had been punctured from his sails. 'She's not loopy, you know. Just had a rather difficult childhood – endless explosives, guns, bombs. Most people don't have those sort of experiences; it's affected her sensibilities.'

'I'm sorry to hear that, I didn't realise they'd endured such dreadful bombardments in Yorkshire.'

'Oh, they didn't – it was the factory behind the house, you see. Always setting something or other off. All that noise, very bad for the nerves.'

'Her father owns his own artillery works, doesn't he?'

'Yes. Made a fortune during the war, although it hasn't changed him a bit. Salt of the earth, the whole family.' Adam grinned, more like his old self.

'Except Gertrude,' I noted.

'Ah, well, yes. But don't you worry, I've got her well in hand. She didn't do it, you know.'

'No, I never thought she did.'

'Really?' His eyebrows shot up. 'That's a relief, old boy. I was a touch concerned that you'd finger her to the Bill. Don't want to see the old girl locked up. Most unfair on her.'

'Don't worry on that score, Adam, no one wants to see her put away.' I nearly added, 'apart from your father', but held my tongue.

'No, no. Because if she were, her pater would see me disinherited on the spot and we can't have that, can we! Anyway, thank you, Lennox. Knew you'd understand, old boy, and if you're ever in a tight spot, you just let me know. I can give you ten per cent, an excellent deal. Won't get better than that!'

He took himself off, rubbing his hands together, happy as a lark. If I ever do resort to murder, Adam will be top of my list – upon which thought I set off for my HQ with the intention of making progress in my enquiries.

I didn't get very far, though: Peregrine Kingsley was waiting for me at the top of the stairs. Marvellous, just what I needed: more bloody Kingsleys.

'Heathcliff,' he started, blue eyes pinning themselves to mine.

I held up my hand and gave him my best glare in return.

'I mean, Lennox.'

'Yes?'

'Gertrude.'

'No.'

'Pardon?'

'She didn't do it and she's not nuts,' I told him quite firmly.

'I think she did and she is,' he replied, just as firmly. 'And you must inform the constabulary and convince them to put her away somewhere safe.'

'No.'

'She cold-bloodedly murdered the Countess, you heard her say it herself, and now she's trying to murder me.' He'd gone a degree paler under that tan of his. His silver hair was dishevelled, and the handkerchief in his top pocket showed signs of use rather than being the perfectly pressed triangle he habitually sported – perhaps he truly was worried. 'And she's stolen my letter-opener. It is formed in the manner of a dagger, solid silver with a gilt-edged handle. Adam swears she doesn't have it but I know she does, and she intends to murder me with it.' His eyes were beginning to take on a boggled aspect.

'I don't believe that for a moment, but if you're so worried inform the damn police yourself.'

'But you have made investigations. You can find proof. They always ask for it – the police. Always.'

'Have you been threatened before?' I leaned in to look him more closely in the face.

He blanched to a further shade of pale. 'Possibly ... It does happen ... there are any number of confused people around.' He took a shot at pulling himself together. 'Look, Lennox, she needs locking up. It's not just last night's episode, there's much more to it than that. She believes me to be among the fallen – debauched! She accused me of it and she thinks I'm going to corrupt Adam, who's a saint in her eyes. It's madness.'

Actually, he could almost convince me on that point, but there's no accounting for love and one could hardly go round locking people up just because they're blinded by tender emotion.

'Peregrine, you cannot advocate incarcerating the poor girl just because she loves your son, however deluded it may seem.'

'But you don't understand – she is deluded. And it would make me feel a lot safer if she were arrested. And it gets you off the hook.' He raised his finger and pointed at me.

'I'm not on the hook – you are!'

'Of course I'm not. I've never heard such a preposterous notion!' Kingsley stepped back as though thoroughly offended, which was highly inappropriate because I hadn't even started being offensive yet. 'I tell you she's going to kill me!' he shouted.

'And why the devil would she do that?' Actually, I could think of any number of reasons, but those mostly arose from my own antipathy toward the man.

He coughed, lowered his voice and fingered his shirt collar. 'It may be related to some investments I advised her father to buy.'

'Wouldn't be the same useless stocks you recommended to me, by any chance?'

'Eastern Railroad. Yes, actually, it was,' Kingsley admitted. 'It was a good opportunity, should have made an excellent return. It was hardly my fault it didn't come off. Can't make money without taking a risk. I made that quite clear at the time.'

'You didn't make it clear to me!' I retorted.

'Slings and arrows and all that, Heath … Lennox,' he corrected himself. 'If it had concluded profitably, you'd have been praising me as your saviour now, wouldn't you?' He looked at me, realised his powers of persuasion were suffering from terminal wilt and changed tack. 'As it happens, the man is suing me. It is the act of an utter philistine, he must realise financial advisers cannot give guarantees, and he understood that my commission was not dependent on the outcome. He is taking a very provincial attitude – city people understand the rules.'

'Are you trying to tell me you made a commission from your advice to me, Kingsley?' I raised my voice to make damn sure that not only he but most of the rest of the house could hear me.

'Lennox, how do you think financiers make money? This is utterly naïve of you,' he shouted back, 'you have no more sense than a country yokel!'

'And you are a charlatan! If you can't make money yourself from the stocks and shares you push onto unsuspecting investors, what sort of damn adviser are you?'

'I'm not going to bandy words with someone so ignorant of the sophisticated complexities of commerce.' With that he turned and stormed off upstairs to the next floor and his own suite of rooms, whence I heard the door take a resounding slam.

A bevy of footmen were standing at the bottom of the stairs looking up. I glowered at them and they dispersed like a gaggle of hens catching sight of a fox. With rage in my breast I returned to my rooms and yanked the bell for Cooper – I needed coffee, strong and black. With biscuits!

Once ensconced in comfort, I calmed and directed my thoughts towards wax. I'd stewed over the puzzle while partaking of my steaming coffee and shortbread, and I'd hit upon the answer: chicken feathers.

Togged up once again for the great outdoors, I made my way to unknown territory at the rear of the house, where the windows gave me gazing rights upon the ceaseless activity of the cogs and wheels of Uncle's country pile.

'Oo're you, then?' Mr Biggs, the butcher, asked while splitting the ribs of a beast with a meat cleaver.

Biggs was a big man: black hair, beard, moustache, with a touch of the Neanderthal about him.

'Major Lennox,' I retorted as the cleaver came thudding down once again.

'From t'ouse?' Thud.

'Yes.' Thud.

'Seen you once.' Thud.

'Could you stop doing that, please?' Thud.

He laid the instrument down on the massive block of wood – sliced, warped and blackened with age and blood and the regular smashing of the axe. The butchery was a fascinating place, and I couldn't think why I'd never been there before. As children, we'd been expressly forbidden to visit, and if there hadn't been other interesting places which we'd been expressly forbidden to visit, I'm sure we'd have thoroughly explored it. Skinned and cleaned carcasses hung from big metal hooks in the beamed ceiling: venison, wild boar, ribs of beef, and whole lambs. From a rail along the whitewashed walls hung trussed geese, ducks, rabbits, hare, pheasant and chickens. Another rack sported strings of sausages, hams and black puddings. A veritable feast for the eyes.

'What d'you want, then?' Biggs leaned closer to me from his great height, wiping his huge, bloodied hands on his huge, bloodied apron.

'To take a look at your wax.'

'Eh?'

'You use wax to clean pin feathers off the fowl, don't you?'

'Aye, always 'ave dun.'

'What sort of wax?' I asked.

He looked at me as though I were thoroughly cooked. 'Eh?'

'Where is it?'

He pointed to a bucket under the grey stone gutting slab. I went over and inspected it, drew out the jam jar I'd collected from the kitchens en route, and, with my slim hunting knife, cut away a chunk of wax and dropped it into the jar. I held it up in front of the barred window – it was whitish, with bits and pieces of feathers and detritus encased in it.

'Has any member of the house come in here asking for wax, Biggs?'

He slowly shook his head.

'Thank you, Biggs,' I remarked on departing. 'Good day.'

He didn't utter a word as I left, just stared at me dumbfounded.

As I made my way back along that self-same path worn in the snow which I had viewed from my window, I mused upon what I had discovered. According to Biggs, none of the house guests had been at his butchery, and when I considered the matter further I had to ask myself which of them would know the country practice of dunking fowl in warm wax to remove pin feathers? And how many would realise where the wax could be found? It wouldn't take long for the police to deduce that the person who was most likely to have concocted the delayed-action firecracker was me.

As my search for paraffin wax had proven more confounding than enlightening, I wanted to take some time in uninterrupted thought, so I decided to take the long way around the house to the front door rather than directly through the kitchens. I traversed the Italian knot garden, the French parterre, and bypassed the ha-ha, before approaching the corner of the east wing deep in thought. Just as I placed my boot on the first step of the raised terrace, I heard a bloodcurdling yell, rapidly followed by a resounding thump as something hit the snow-covered paving just ahead of me.

I reached the cause in short order and stared down.

Damn it, this was the third time in a week. The glazed eyes of a very dead body stared up at the wintery sky, blood trickling from the side of the gaping mouth. Peregrine Kingsley lay spreadeagled in the snow, and it was very evident he had breathed his last.

CHAPTER 15

It was a futile gesture, but I bent over him and checked for a pulse on the remote chance he might not be quite as deceased as he appeared. Unhappily for him, he was. I straightened up as a man in a rumpled hat, gardening garb and closely resembling a bandy-legged gnome came dashing up to me, goggle-eyed with shock.

'Ee, by God,' he panted as he halted beside the defunct Kingsley. 'Is 'e dead, then?'

'I'm afraid he is,' I replied coolly. Not that I was unfeeling, but finding dead bodies in unexpected places was becoming rather commonplace.

'Yer sure, then?' the gardener asked. ''E's gone?'

'I am. I've seen a lot of them. He is.'

'Well, I'll be blowed. Are ye one of the 'ouse, then?'

I nodded. 'I assume you to be one of the garden?'

'Ay, I yam that. I be Tom.'

'Lennox,' I reciprocated.

I looked up at the house, trying to gauge where Kingsley had fallen from. Tom followed my gaze.

'Up there, look. Windo's open, d'ye see?'

'Ah, yes. Third floor. It'll be one of the spare bedrooms, or possibly a corridor.'

We both looked down at Kingsley again, lying in the snow like a fallen angel – well, fallen, anyway. I suddenly thought about the time and tugged out my fob watch.

'Must have happened about three. It's two minutes after now,' I said.

Tom took a step back, staring up at me. 'Ee, tha's clever of you.'

'What?'

'Thinkin' about the time. Like in those detective stories. You a detective, then?'

'No,' I told him, 'but I'm learning about it,' I added, with some little pride. 'Getting quite a lot of practice, actually.'

'D'ye think 'e jumped?'

'No.'

''E were murdered, then?' Tom asked in a voice of awe and shock with a frisson of excitement.

'I'm afraid so.'

'It's goin' to cause a right to-do, this is,' Tom uttered. 'Murdered. An 'e's a gent, so 'e is.' He stared down at Kingsley's recumbent form.

'Indeed, yes. Well, of sorts,' I agreed, and clapped my hands, rubbing them together to get the blood moving. 'Right, you stay here, Tom, and I'll go and find somebody to call the police.'

'Ay, I'll be doing that, Mr Lennox.'

'Major,' I corrected him.

'Ay, Mr Major.'

I departed at a run in search of Cooper or anyone else of sense in the house. I found Cartwright instead.

'Don't say a word, Cartwright. Just go and get Cooper and tell him to come here immediately.'

He opened his mouth to reply, but I pointed sternly and shouted, 'Go!' and he went.

Then I rang the gong, giving it a good thump three times, and then another three. That should get some attention.

Edgar was the first to peer down over the balustrade at me.

'I need your help, old man.'

He raced down. 'What? Tell me – is it Uncle?'

'No: Peregrine. Dead.' I said sotto voce. 'He's on the terrace.'

Cooper came from wherever he'd been. 'Sir?'

'Police. Please call them.'

Edgar was looking shocked. 'What happened?'

'Certainly, sir. May I enquire why, sir?'

'Another death. I'm trying not to cause too much alarm,' I told him.

'Well, why did you bang the gong, then?' Edgar asked. 'You'll have the whole house here shortly.'

He was right about that: a number of footmen had already come into the hall and Cooper turned to order them back to their duties. Uncle appeared at the top of the stairs, and then Natasha came to join him.

'Wait there, we're coming up,' I shouted.

Cooper had already taken command and was telephoning for the police with one hand and redirecting servants with the other as Edgar and I raced upstairs.

'Natasha,' I ordered her, 'take Uncle to his rooms, or somewhere. Ring for some tea. Calm him down.'

'I am calm and I don't want to go to my rooms,' Uncle said. 'Why did you ring the gong?'

'Yes,' Natasha joined. 'Why?'

'There's been a tragic accident,' Edgar told them.

'Yes, excellent explanation!' I added. 'A tragic accident. Someone threw Peregrine out of a window.'

'Oh, no,' Natasha cried, and fainted to the floor – I wished she wouldn't do that. Edgar knelt and did his best to revive her, holding her hand and whatnot.

'No!' Uncle exclaimed, hand flying to his mouth, eyebrows shooting up his forehead.

Adam came down from the second floor with Gertrude following three steps behind. Things were getting tricky.

'What happened? Why was the gong sounded?' Adam asked.

I realised then that I may have overreacted with the gong. Fortunately, Cooper was coming up from the hall.

'Cooper, you take charge. I'm going to search the house,' I ordered, and dashed off to the third floor of the east wing to find the open window. I was also keen to distance myself from uncomfortable revelations to Adam.

The cold draught led me to it pretty quickly, and I shouted down to Tom from the open window while taking great care not to touch anything in case of fingerprints.

'There'll be someone coming soon,' I called to where he was still diligently standing by Kingsley's cadaver.

'Right you are, Mr Major,' he called back with a cheery wave.

The sash window was at the very end of a passage in an unused part of the house. There was a closed door leading to the back stairs so I opened the brass knob with a handkerchief and had a look around without crossing the threshold. A small landing led to a set of plain pine stairs with a dark handrail, between whitewashed walls in need of a fresh coat of paint. It didn't seem very enlightening, so I closed it.

I stood back, rubbing my jaw. It was a lonely spot, ideal for a meeting because nobody would come here by chance. The bottom sill was at knee height; anyone leaning over could easily unbalance. I looked again and made a deduction: Peregrine knew his killer; they'd persuaded him to lean out of the window on some excuse, and then simply pushed him out.

I moved back closer to the window, peering closely at the frame – it was also white and in need of a fresh coat of paint. The inside edge had a couple of chips knocked off, which appeared newly made. I could make out little flakes of paint around the damage, and a couple on the floor. A thin dark mark was evident – such as the sole of a shoe would leave as its owner hurtled to their end, though I couldn't be sure whether it mightn't in fact be a figment of my overactive deductive imagination. I may have to invest in a proper magnifying glass if people keep dying like this.

Apart from that, there was nothing there: no sign of a struggle, no curtains to be ripped off or torn down, no furniture to grab, no carpet to catch hairs – just a poorly polished parquet floor. I glanced up at the ceiling, which was undisturbed, although a brief flash of something shiny caught the light on the lower rail of the open sash. I twisted my neck to look at it: a smear of grease. It had a faint scent, like hair oil.

Did Kingsley wear hair oil? Not that I could recall; and he was probably too soggy now to be certain.

But Adam did, and Edgar did. I recoiled – it was most likely one of them!

At that moment Edgar came up behind me, making me jump. I swung around to face him.

'Lennox, how the devil did it happen?' He went directly to the window and peered out, hands firmly held behind his back to avoid touching anything, then he stepped backwards and quickly surveyed the area – he seemed very cognisant of this sort of procedure.

'Do you think he fell?'

'No.' I told him my conclusions about his being pushed.

'You're sure? I mean, he might have fallen if someone were calling to him from the garden, say.'

'He'd have to be a complete idiot to fall out of a window, even this one. Anyway, why would he be here in the first place? It's nowhere near his rooms, or anywhere, really.'

'Yes, that's a good point.' Edgar looked around again, then opened the door to the back stairs with a handkerchief as I had done, peered in and shut the door again. 'Needs a coat of paint.'

'Yes. Are the police coming?'

'Cooper said they would try, but it depends on the snow. The Inspector gave very explicit instructions – nobody is to move the body and he has to be covered up. He mustn't be touched either.' Edgar eyed me closely. 'You didn't, did you, old man?'

'Well, I felt for a pulse, but that's all.'

'I meant you didn't push him out, did you?'

'Good God no!' I exclaimed, rather hurt that he'd asked. 'Why should I?'

'Well, you had a tremendous ballyhoo with him this morning, everyone heard it.'

'I was in the garden when he fell, and I have a witness. He's called Tom. He saw it all, just after I did.'

I told him briefly what happened, not bothering to fill him in about Mr Biggs, the wax or the hair oil, which would just confuse matters (well, it had confused me, anyway).

'How's Uncle?' I asked.

'Oh, he's fine. Getting used to it now, I think.'

'Excellent! What about Natasha?'

'Taking tea with Uncle in the drawing room. Cooper is making a fuss of them. And I gave her the smelling salts from last time, in case she feels the need.'

'Good, good – and Adam? I suppose he must be pretty cut up?'

'He looked rather surprised when I told him.'

'Not upset or guilty or pleased?'

'This is Adam we're talking about – he may have been any of those. I asked Gertrude to take him for a lie-down, and she asked why. Cooper managed to persuade her in the end – something about "under the auspices of angels".'

'Do you want to come and have a look at him? Peregrine, I mean?' I asked.

'Good idea, yes. I'll pick up my boots and coat in the hall. Is it very cold out?'

'Indeed it is. The snow is thawing, but I'd wear gloves and a hat, too, if I were you.'

Thus, convulsed with sorrow for our departed relative, we went off to examine his remains.

We trudged through the slush to the gnomish figure of Tom and the splayed body of Kingsley in the melting snow.

'Hello, Tom,' I said, 'this is Mr Edgar.'

'All right there guv'nor; an' Mr Major.' Tom nodded to us both. The days of doffing caps appeared to be over, as he made no attempt to pull the grubby object from his head.

'I'm Major Lennox, Tom. Not Mr Major.'

'Well, why'd ye say –'

I held up my hand. 'Let's concentrate on the matter in hand, shall we? Would you please tell Mr Edgar what you saw?'

'This gent down 'ere –' he pointed to Peregrine '– fell from up there.' He pointed to the upper floors of the house.

'Did you see him fall?' Edgar asked.

'No.'

'Did you see him land?'

'No.'

'So, what alerted you to the event?' I interrupted, since Edgar was getting nowhere.

'I 'eard a sort of blood-curdlin' yell, like a soul starin' into the face o' the devil 'imself. Then I 'eard a thud, like a sack o' spuds droppin' into a well that didn't 'ave no water in it, on account of it bein' all froze to ice, so it just went scrunch, like.'

'Erm, yes. Very picturesque description, Tom,' I said by way of congratulation.

'I'm a well-read man, ye know. Read a lot o' books, I do. From the market. Penny a book. Can't get better than that, can you?'

'Um, no, no. Excellent,' I said. 'Right. Now you will have to remain here, Tom. The police have asked that the body be attended at all times. I suppose we'll have to cover it up, too.'

'An umbrella an' a bale o' straw'll do the trick, Mr Major Lennox. You just 'ave someone sends 'em out an' I'll be right as rain.'

'Very well, Tom, it will be arranged,' I promised him,' and by the way, it's ...' He regarded me, open-mouthed and toothless. 'No, never mind.'

We scrutinised the late Kingsley once more. He looked even deader than before, having gone quite grey and with an expression on his face that is probably best described as aghast.

We dropped off our outdoor vestments, nipped to the kitchens to warm up and sample some mulled wine and returned to the third floor for further investigations. I peered out to see Tom comfortably seated upon a straw bale holding an umbrella over Kingsley with one hand and reading a pocket-sized book with the other.

Edgar had armed himself with a magnifying glass the better to observe the back stairs. It availed us nought. There was a thin layer of undisturbed dust on the stair-treads, proving that no one had been up or down for some considerable time. A dead-end, I concluded, and dropped to my hands and knees for a closer inspection of the paint chips from the window sill, thus confirming that they were indeed paint chips. I plucked one up with tweezers and placed it carefully in a jam jar brought for the very purpose.

Then we stared at the scrape on the paintwork; it could have been made by Peregrine's shoe, but without the actual item for comparison it was guesswork.

'To sum up,' I told Edgar, 'we have discovered not very much, except that at three o'clock this afternoon he fell, or was more likely pushed, from this window.'

'Defenestration,' he replied.

'What?'

'Death by defenestration, that's what it's called.'

'You mean there's a word for it?' I was incredulous.

'Yes, and in fact it's a very popular means of murder, particularly in foreign parts, where stuffing people out of windows is quite the norm.'

'Some of the foreign parts I've been to didn't have windows; some of them didn't even have walls.'

'Yes, Lennox, but there was a war raging at the time.'

'I'm not going again, you know. Abroad, I mean. Awful place: no one understands English, the food's dire, there are rats, bombs and lashings of mud. Stuff got everywhere. Awful,' I said with feeling. And then: 'I think it's going to freeze.'

'What?'

'The weather, the draught from the window. The wind's turned north.'

'Lennox, could we just stick to the subject.'

'Which one?'

'I have no idea, you keep shooting off on tangents!' He sounded unnecessarily exasperated.

'It's getting dark. We can't leave Tom out there all night, we'll end up with two corpses by morning.'

'You think the police won't be able to get through today?'

'No, not given the change in the weather. Listen, Edgar, would you telephone Inspector Swift and ask for permission to remove the body to one of the outbuildings? There's a butchery in the rear courtyard, Peregrine could be left in one of the store-rooms.'

Edgar thought about it, hand under his chin, staring

out at the horizon, where heavy grey clouds were already rolling in.

'Yes, very well – but on your head be it.'

We returned to the hall and Edgar went on his way to the telephone in its small nook under the staircase. I listened to him shouting at the operator, then I accosted Cooper, who was looking somewhat frazzled by the fuss.

'Need a guard, or screens, rope,' I told him.

'Pardon, sir?'

'For the window where Kingsley was defenestrated.'

He looked at me as though entirely baffled. 'Pardon, sir?'

'Cooper.' I began again as his wits had apparently wandered off somewhere else entirely. 'Please either provide a person to guard the window from which Sir Peregrine fell, or rope it off or screen it, or something akin.'

'Ah! Yes, sir, I see, sir.'

'Oh, and ensure that the door to the back stairs is locked too, would you?'

'Very good, sir.'

He went off, leaving me to wonder if the Countess may have had a point about the old butler being ready for pasture. With that thought in mind, I drifted off to the drawing room to see how Uncle was bearing up.

'Greetings, dear Uncle,' I accosted him on arrival. He was sitting in front of the fire, accompanied only by Mr Fogg, who was staring intently at the tray at Uncle's elbow, which still supported a number of Cook's very best shortbread biscuits.

I snaffled one and broke it in half to share with my dog. 'Any coffee left?'

'I think so. Should I ring for Cooper?'

'No need, I can manage.'

The tray had been part of the afternoon tea ritual, and on the sideboard lay many more dainty offerings as well as coffee. I poured myself one and plumped myself down opposite him.

'I never liked him, you know,' Uncle said, looking at me with gentle eyes behind eyebrows reminiscent of a knotted sheep.

'Kingsley? No one did. Why on earth have you allowed him to leech off you all these years, Uncle? He's been hanging around here like a bloodsucking bat for as long as I can remember.'

'He rather came with the place,' Uncle sighed. 'When my father died I wasn't interested in the house at all. Your Aunt Mary and I were still in India, part of the British Raj, you recall. Wonderful times they were.' He lapsed into momentary reverie, then set off again. 'Peregrine had worked alongside his father looking after the estate and I left them to it. By the time we came home his father had died and Peregrine had woven himself into the very cobwebs. He knew every detail, every transaction, all the little problems, and acted as though he had all the solutions.' He stopped to sip his coffee. 'I suppose it was rather cowardly of me to let him continue. We didn't trust him, Mary and I, but he made us feel very ignorant and incapable of overseeing this huge domain ourselves.

As Mary's health continued to deteriorate, I simply left it to him. I was never able to unpick the tentacles he'd spread throughout the place.'

'Were you attracted to the Countess because you knew she would remove him?' I asked.

'Yes – frankly, that was one of her many attractions. I knew she wouldn't tolerate his interference.'

'There were safer ways to get rid of Kingsley than marrying Sophia, Uncle – and I doubt she was going to tolerate any of us.'

'I realise that now. But she was dazzling, so very vibrant and alive. I felt energised by her presence. I will miss her, you know. Even though she would have proven overbearing in the end, it would have been an exciting ride.' His face lit up as he talked, eyes shining.

'There's a lot to uncover about Sophia,' I commented dryly.

'Yes, I was looking forward to uncovering the lady myself,' Uncle muttered.

I glanced sideways at him with raised eyebrows; he was staring into the fire with a grin on his face. I coughed, but he was oblivious, so I poured another cup of coffee each and passed one to him.

'Natasha,' I said.

'Ah yes. Pretty girl, nice manners. You know she and Edgar are engaged?'

'Of course. I'm to be the best man.'

'I'm not sure about it.' He shook his head.

'Really, why so?'

'He's looking for a wife – any wife. That's not a good reason for getting wed.'

'It's as good as any. Edgar's never going to fall in love so why not choose a partner who'll be an asset. And she is an asset: well educated, well travelled, charming when she wants to be, highly decorative, and no peculiar relatives likely to turn up and make a nuisance of themselves.' Knowing Edgar, this was just the sort of assessment he'd have made before popping the question.

'He might fall in love one day. These emotions are not to be taken lightly, Heathcliff.'

Considering the path love had almost led Uncle down, I think Edgar's cool logic made a damn sight more sense than the random firing of fickle feelings. The topic had wandered off track and I sought to divert it back.

'When I said Natasha, I meant that she's the most likely route to lifting the veil on Sophia's secrets.'

'Ah yes, well, she may be.' Uncle looked at me, suddenly serious. 'I've tried asking her myself, but she finds excuses. You need to talk to her, Heathcliff. And I mean talk, don't allow her any evasions.' He thumped his walking stick on the carpet as he said this. 'I really do think you must get to the bottom of this necklace business; that is the cause of all the mayhem.' He pointed a wrinkled finger at me now. 'And I don't wish to cast aspersions, my boy, but you started it all and you must finish it, or we'll have more deaths, and one of them might be mine.'

I must say, I thought that dashed unfair. I was the one who had been defrauded by his damn fiancée – how was it all my fault? But I held my tongue; the old man was upset and probably frightened.

'Uncle Charles –' I looked him in the eyes '– I promise I will do my best.'

'And so you must, Heathcliff. Lives depend upon it.'

CHAPTER 16

I can't say my blood was boiling, but it was pretty warm when I embarked on my mission to uncover the blighter responsible for disposing of two people I didn't particularly like before they managed to murder someone I did.

First stop was a place I'd been studiously avoiding, my old rooms and until very recently the Countess's suite. The door was locked, the key wasn't on the lintel and I had to fumble around in my pockets to produce my own. I ignored the sign on the door, 'POLICE NOTICE, DO NOT ENTER', and flicked on the lights.

It was awful, I could barely believe my eyes. The place was festooned with cushions in shiny fabrics; every chair held one or more. And the chairs weren't even mine – they were fussy items requisitioned from other rooms in the house along with spindly sofas, alabaster lamps, marble-topped tables, Aubusson tapestries and some of the best oil paintings Uncle owned, including my favourite Stubbs. Silk rugs littered the carpet and the whole place stank of her perfume. It stopped me dead in my tracks and I briefly mourned my old nest before deciding

I'd have the whole lot thrown out in the morning and returned to its habitual shabby homeliness.

I stalked around the place horror-struck, then gave myself a good ticking off. I was supposed to be searching for clues, things of significance, not fretting over the Countess's hideous taste in decor. The police had left evidence of their presence – fingerprint powder was scattered on all the furniture, the mantelpiece, and indeed anything it could be thrown at. I paused to look more closely at the sideboard – the decanters and glasses all showed smears, prints and marks. I assumed the police would know which belonged to whom, but it didn't help me as I hadn't got anyone's fingerprints. I could ask, I supposed, but it would probably be met with cries of outrage and refusal.

The bedroom had been transformed even more horribly, and one look in the drawers at some of Sophia's nether-garments caused me to retreat rapidly to the sitting room. It looked as if I was going to have to exit empty-handed – but then I thought to have a probe around in the ashes of the fire. It had probably been alight on the night of the murder, and given the main focus on the drawing room, might not yet have been inspected. There were probably rules about interfering with evidence, but if I let minor details like that stop me, I'd never achieve anything.

I poked around with my pen among the logs and carbonised coal. Right at the back lay the balled-up remains of the telegram – gave me quite a thrill to find it, actually.

It was badly charred, and blackened flakes fell off as I fished it out of the detritus and carefully rolled it onto the hearth.

Damn it. Every time I tried to unwrap it another bit fell off. It was too tightly wound to flatten out and the actual message was the bit that was most burned. But as I manoeuvred it around, I could make out writing scrawled on the back – something that Cartwright probably hadn't even been aware of. I took out the flashlight Edgar had given me for Christmas and shone it on the blackened paper. It was an address, and one that I knew very well because it was in Eaton Square: it was Edgar's address.

I recoiled in shock, my mind churning through the implications, and then pulled myself together – no point in losing my head when I didn't know the facts. I extracted a jam jar from my pocket, which I'd brought with me, along with my tweezers, then dropped the crumbling paper into it and stood up. I'd had enough for one day, so I returned to the Blue rooms rather churned up and feeling a bit like a voyeur.

Once back at my HQ I resumed my seat behind my desk and took up pen and notebook. What did I make of it? The ink dried on the nib as I sat in a funk; wind blowing a gale against the windows, hail and snow spitting a tattoo, like machine-gun fire from foreign trenches. It couldn't be Edgar; I just couldn't accept that possibility. I thought back over the last few days, and the wheres and whyfores of our movements and conversations. Thankfully the dinner gong sounded to snap me from my thoughts and I dropped the pen, shut up my notebook and made my way down to the dining room.

The table was set for six, the candles were lit, the servants were in their places, but no one else had arrived. I took my seat as Cooper poured wine into my glass.

'Where's His Lordship, Cooper?' I asked.

'Eating a light supper in his rooms, sir.'

A footman placed a bowl of soup in front of me.

'And Mr Edgar?'

'Accompanying Miss Natasha, taking a meal in her rooms, sir.'

I raised my spoon.

'And the remaining Kingsleys?'

'Also partaking of supper in their suite, sir.'

I spooned my soup and dunked my bread, still warm from the oven. Dash it, I could eat alone – I did it all the time!

I returned to my rooms after a hearty meal, feeling much better. There was bound to be a good explanation for Edgar's seeming involvement in all of this, and tomorrow after a good sleep I would winkle it out.

First thing I noticed on opening my eyes was my breath rising white above the bedcovers: the temperature had dropped in the night. I tossed aside the covers and went to light the fire, having woken before any maids or minions had come to perform their duties ahead of me. I stoked it up until it was brightly blazing, then threw open the curtains to peer at the ice on the inside of the panes and rubbed a clear circle to give me a spy-hole on the world. It was white and frosty and absolutely freezing. It also meant we would be police-free for another day; the roads were not just impassable now, they were deadly. Yesterday's melting slush would have turned glacial overnight and a topping of snow in the early hours would make a dangerous combination. Standing up on such a surface would be hazardous, never mind trying to take a vehicle onto it.

Fogg refused to remove himself from his nest in the bedcovers, so I pulled on my new dressing gown, tucked my recalcitrant dog under my arm and went downstairs to dump him outside on the doorstep. He stared up at me, shivered, then trotted down the steps until his feet lost their purchase and he slid down on his backside to the bottom. Poor dog threw me an accusing glare before taking a short pee and then scrambling back up and into the house. I followed as fast as I could; it really was agonisingly cold.

Contemplating the day over my breakfast tray, I decided to adhere to my plan to corner Natasha and compel her to open up about Aunty and the necklace. Then I'd be better armed to confront Edgar with actual facts rather than a mishmash of confused evidence and coincidences. But first there was something else I wanted to do – I needed to visit one of my favourite places in the house, the gunroom.

Unfortunately, much as I liked the gunroom, I had never seen eye to eye with its incumbent, Lurch. (His name wasn't actually Lurch, it was Luther, but he'd lost a leg in some remote war, and to me and Edgar he'd always been Lurch. He didn't much care for us either.)

'Lurch,' I greeted him.

'Humph.' He pivoted on his wooden leg to glare at me, then swivelled back again.

'And a jolly good morning to you, too,' I said.

He was standing at the workbench, thin winter sunshine streaming in from the windows onto the vice, in which the long barrel of an ancient rifle was clamped. It was difficult to see much of his face, since he sported a huge black and grey beard topped with a moustache and his hair stuck out at angles – he looked like he was wearing an enraged skunk. His eyes held a similar expression, though it was quite hard to tell under his thatch of brows.

'I have a question for you.' I addressed his back, as he hadn't seen fit to turn around.

'Humph,' was the only response I got; then he started filing the gun barrel noisily.

'Have any firecrackers gone missing?' I shouted above the screeching racket.

He stopped a moment, file held in grimy hand, then turned round and glared at me.

'What sort?' he growled, his voice as rough as the file in his fist.

'Any sort, really. Is anything missing?' I was trying to be polite, but it was entirely lost on the man.

'The police were in here. Poking around.' He pivoted back to the workbench and started filing again.

'Please stop doing that, Lurch.'

But Lurch carried on until he'd finished, at which point he laid the file down and pivoted back to look me squarely in the eye.

'It's not right.'

'What isn't?'

'Police. If you hadn't shot that old woman, I wouldn't have had police in here. Made a right mess, they did.'

'I didn't shoot her. Ask Cooper. Ask anyone. If I'd shot her, I'd be in gaol now.'

'Why?'

'Because that's what they do if you shoot people.'

'She was foreign.'

'It doesn't matter, they still put you in gaol.'

'I shot a lot of foreigners. And they shot me. Lost me leg thanks to foreigners, I did. Didn't put me in gaol, gave me a medal.'

'You're allowed to shoot them abroad. I mean, you can when there's a war on. Anyway, I didn't come to talk about shooting because I didn't shoot her.'

'Who did then?'

'I've no idea. Well, I might have an inkling, but I'm not telling you. Look, Lurch, did anything go missing?'

'Ay.'

'What?'

'Small bomb.'

'Really?'

'Just said, didn't I?'

'Yes, yes … I didn't know we had any bombs.'

'From the last war. Home Defence. Had a lot of them

around here. They was practising shooting, an' all. I found a good lot of stuff in their stores, so I did.'

There was no point in asking him why he was looting their stores or I'd be here all day.

'What sort of small bomb went missing?'

'M-80.'

'Oh.' I nodded. 'Why do you have them?'

'Why not? Might come in useful one day. Always something needs blowin' up. A couple of dozen would do the trick.' At this, a note of enthusiasm sounded in his usual dour tone.

'So how many were stolen?'

'All of them.'

'Good God! The murderer could bring the whole damn house down around our ears.' This was startling news. I had better do something.

'Don't be so daft, lad. One went missing just afore Christmas. It were the police took the rest.'

'Ah. That's a relief. Why the blazes didn't you say so?'

'I did, didn't I. You wasn't listening.' He pivoted back to his workbench, picked up the file and started rasping the barrel again.

I left, having better things to do than be ignored by Lurch.

Once back at my HQ I wrote, 'Bang: M-80 with delayed fuse caused by paraffin-wax coating.'

M-80s made one hell of a racket; they were used by the Army to simulate the sound of gunfire – perfect for the subterfuge set up by the murderer. I considered listing the names of people who would know what they were and how to use them, but since that was just about everyone, I didn't bother.

Lunch beckoned, as did my meeting with Natasha. I trotted off in the direction of the dining room for a heartening meal and to lay an ambush for the girl. I did this by cornering Cooper and giving him instructions to redirect everyone else to the morning room, thus ensuring it would just be me and Natasha for a quiet tête-à-tête. It was quite some time before she turned up, and after my fine repast I wasted a good half hour trying to make sense of a three-day-old copy of the *Financial Times*.

'Good day,' I offered in greeting.

She eyed me warily and came to a halt beside her usual chair, but didn't sit down. She'd noticed immediately there was no one else present; nor was the table set, and it put her on her guard.

'Natasha, I need to talk to you,' I began. 'And you need to talk to me.'

Her eyes flicked across to the windows, where ice was stuck to the panes. She wore a pale-blue silk dress trimmed with white lace, and a long string of creamy pearls about her neck. She really was a very attractive girl – the very epitome of elegance and class.

'When?'

'Now, please. Sit down. I've given orders that we are not to be disturbed. Would you like to eat first?'

'No, I find I am without hunger.

She sat in her chair, smoothing her dress beneath her

with a sweep of her hand before settling straight-backed upon the seat. I rested my elbows on the table, notebook in front of me and pen in hand. I intended to run this interview properly, the way Swift did.

'Where were you at three o'clock yesterday afternoon when Peregrine fell from the window?' I began.

'In my rooms. Where were you?'

'Um ...' I was sure interviewees weren't supposed to answer back like that. 'In the garden, with Tom. Well, not with him, but I was there at the same time as him. Anyway,' I regrouped, 'who was with you?'

'No one,' Natasha replied coolly. 'I was writing my journal, as I do most afternoons.'

'Really? That's impressive, I've never managed more than a couple of days. Have you always kept one?'

'No, I started when we left Russia. This is a new life for me, I must understand your ways, such as not having peasants and yokels, which are called farmer folk. I want to try to, how you say, get a grip of it.'

I stared down at my notebook – I wasn't getting a grip on anything. 'Natasha. Your aunt wasn't your aunt, was she?'

Ha! That shook her. Her eyes flew wide open, her mouth dropped for a split second, then she closed it into a hard tight line before answering.

'How do you know this?'

'I may not know much about Russian aristocracy, but I can spot class when I see it. Nothing about Sophia's choices spoke of nobility, elegance or, frankly, any discernment at all. Whereas you must have inhaled refinement from birth. My mother was the same, so are most people I know. Sophia had none of that.'

She turned to gaze toward the windows again, as if wanting to be far away.

I continued to press her. 'You and your "aunt" are from different ends of the spectrum. What was she, a servant of some sort?'

'She was my nanny. While I grew up, she looked after me.' Natasha turned to face me, her face hard and cold.

'And she saved you? When the soldiers came?'

'Yes.' She nodded. 'Everyone was killed, there was a mob battering down the doors of my rooms. I had locked them, barricaded myself in, but I knew they would succeed in breaking them down. Then Sophia came in from the old nursery, from the servants' stairs. I had never used them, never thought about them. I was ready to shoot myself to prevent the mob from catching me. I held the gun in my hand, but she appeared, calling me, telling me to run with her. She said she would care for me as she always had.' Her voice caught on a sob as she finished her story.

I got up and pulled out a napkin from the sideboard drawer and handed it to her. She sniffed into it, and I felt like a snake. I'd just made her re-live a horrific trauma – but then I thought of Edgar and the murders, and knew I had to go on.

'Please tell me what happened next.'

'We hid in the attics. It was our main family home,

much bigger than this one. Sophia led me to the servants' quarters and found me a uniform such as the maids wore. She cut my hair so it was ragged, and my nails, in case they found us. We stayed there for two days until the mob had ransacked the house and were so drunk they were not conscious – the wretched beasts. We escaped from the kitchens wearing horrible clothes and clogs on our feet; I thought we should go to our neighbours, but Sophia said everyone was under attack and they were probably dead too.'

'And so you fled the country?'

'We did, although it took a very long time. We travelled first to Petrograd and found some of my old friends. They were White Russians, just as we were. They were fighting, trying to stave off the Bolsheviks and start a counter-revolution, but after some months they lost. There was another battle, then it was over and Sophia made me run away with her because she said we would never be safe and I think she was right.'

'You went to Paris?'

'We did,' she nodded. 'Many other White Russians made their homes there, too. I felt as though we were among friends again, people like us … but it began to upset Sophia.'

'Why?'

'Because they guessed – the other exiles: they knew she was not of high birth, however hard she tried. She practised her manners and her voice, copied my movements and gestures. I helped her learn. How to comport oneself, how to respond to a bow, how to walk, talk, what to wear. But she was herself, always herself; she was too … how you say … too flamboyant. She loved to dress up, to wear jewels, to play the high lady. But when they made fun of her, I said it cannot work and we must go. So we came to London, where there were not so many Russian nobles and she could act the grand lady without being guessed at. We met Edgar and then Lord Melrose and our lives became possible. We had hope of a future.'

'But why did you remain with her? You are of high birth, you must have known some of those people from the past. They could have helped, acted as a family to you.'

'Sophia held all the gold. She found my father's reserve of gold before we fled the house. I had nothing, she had it all.'

'But surely it was yours.'

'How was I to go on without her? What should I do? Should I steal it from her and flee? No, I could not do it, she had saved my life and so we were tied together and she became my aunt, the Countess, just as my real-life aunt had been.'

'So you did have an Aunt Sophia?'

'Yes. She became a recluse after her husband and son died in the old war. A lady without a man in Russia is almost invisible, so she was placed in one of the family homes until she died. Sophia took her title and tried to convince our fellow exiles – but it could not work.'

I had put down my pen and notepaper by now and was simply conversing with Natasha, quite enthralled by her story.

'Once you were in London, did she cultivate Uncle or did she have genuine feelings for him?'

'I think both, but she would not confide in me. She had changed, I realised. She became transfixed by the idea of becoming a noble lady, of truly being an aristocrat, not just a pretend. This is why she purchased the jewels – because she believed her future rested upon this lie she had created for herself.'

'So you know about the fraud? That she purchased the ruby necklace with a fake bank draft?'

Natasha nodded as a shaft of thin sunlight suddenly emerged from the clouds, shining through the frozen window glass to illuminate the deep dark red of her hair.

'It was not the only occasion, there were others. I told her that the English police would find her out, but she thought it was like Russia here. That the nobles could do whatever they wished and the authorities were little men, just officials to be bought or threatened or simply removed. I warned her, but she paid no heed,' she shook her head at the memory. 'The ruby necklace was special, it was from Macedonia and a great prize in our country; only a grand lady would possess such a thing. Sophia became obsessed with it, her conversation was about it always. I could not listen to her any more – and besides, I had met Edgar. I liked him very much.'

'Were you living in Edgar's apartment? In Eaton Square?'

'Yes, He had allowed us to reside there while he was out in the world with his work. It was a great kindness; we had little money left, we could not pay rent for our flat in London, so I accepted Edgar's offer. Your uncle had proposed to Sophia – she was so very happy, so jubilant, and she had to have the necklace. She said it would help convince him she was a great lady, but I think really she just wanted the ruby.'

I leaned back in my chair to regard her as she regarded me, her face frank and open, her grey eyes gazing into mine with intelligence and the cool hauteur that so patently betrayed her birth.

'Do you know a fat man? I mean really huge, couldn't mistake him. Sophia knew him, used him, I think.'

'The one that died? Edgar told me of a fat man who died.'

'Damn it, he shouldn't have told you that.'

'We are to be husband and wife, why would he not talk to me of such things? And please do not use such abhorrent language.'

'Um, yes, of course. I apologise, Natasha.' Well, that had told me. If I wasn't careful, she'd end up running this interview. 'Erm, would you like something to eat? I can ring for Cooper.'

She nodded in that elegant manner she had and I pulled the bell for attention. It was some little time later after Cooper had furnished Natasha with tea and small sandwiches to encourage her appetite and I had stoked up the fire to fend off the cold draughts that were a feature of every English house in the winter.

'Did Edgar tell you about the fat man before or after

your aunt died?' I hesitated and back-tracked: 'I mean Sophia, of course; your nurse, nanny, whatever she was.'

'After.'

I opened my notebook and asked the question that had trundled around in my mind ever since Greggs had announced the death on my doorstep.

'And who was the fat man? Do you know his name?'

'No. He may have been an acquaintance of Sophia's. She made use of people.'

'What sort of use?' I asked, disappointed that I still hadn't uncovered that particular mystery.

'I think she could have used him when she was purchasing her gems.'

'You knew Sophia was defrauding people?' I asked.

'I knew she was buying jewellery. She wore so many gems, it was ridiculous. We had words and she admitted what she was doing. Eventually there was talk among the few friends we had made in London. She panicked, thinking your uncle would hear of it, so she began to repay those she had defrauded. She must have raised real bank drafts and had them sent to those unfortunates with a note to say it had been a mistake. I suppose your fat man was sent as a messenger. But perhaps he died before he could do so?'

'I imagine so,' I agreed, then thought it over. It was the very conclusion I had come to: the draft had been stolen along with the hat by the driver of the car. It was a disappointing end to my questioning, but it did confirm my hope that Edgar had merely loaned his home to the ladies when they were patently in distress, and hadn't personally directed the fat man. I didn't understand, though, why the devil he hadn't merely told me all this.

'Sophia must have been shocked to discover that I was the owner of the ruby necklace.'

'I do not know. By this time I did not speak to her of such things,' she said shrugging.

We had come to an end, so I stood to escort her from the room. She walked ahead of me, head held high, grace in her every movement.

With slow steps I took myself off for some quiet contemplation. I'd scribbled in my notebook but it was hasty and virtually incoherent; in future I had to be more precise. I had to learn new ways, just as Natasha had.

CHAPTER 17

Once back in my rooms I reached for the bell pull. Foggy followed on my heels and we settled in front of the fire, which I'd just jollied along into blazing glory when Cartwright strolled in with a tray.

'Where's Cooper?' I enquired as he plonked the tea tray down on my desk with a thud, causing the cup to topple onto its saucer.

'There were a call on the telephone, sir. The police it were, upset on account of the weather, which has left them stuck and helpless. They wanted to know what happened to the body of the bloke what got tossed out of the window yesterday. So Mr Cooper had to go and have a look at him to make sure as no one had hidden him nor nothing.'

'Why would anyone want to hide him?'

'Cause they did it, didn't they! Thought you was supposed to be some sort of detective, like the police, but not official.'

'Who said that?'

'Everyone! It's the talk of the house, it is. Some says you

couldn't find your way out of a haystack, but I reckon you're not as daft as you look.'

'Thank you for the dubious compliment, Cartwright. Where were you yesterday at three o'clock?'

'Are you thinking I'm a suspect, then? Ha, ha, I'll be telling that to the others, I will. Me! A suspect in murder, and of a gent, too.'

'Will you just tell me, man?' I poured my own cup as I really dislike cold tea and Cartwright was occupied in irritating chatter and seemed disinclined to do anything of use just at that moment.

'Me and the others was in the Servants' Hall taking our afternoon tisane. We always have it at three – except for when we didn't on account of Her Ladyship.'

'Which Ladyship, Cartwright?'

'The foreign one, that one that got herself shot dead; she changed it, she did. Always had it at three, then she changed the gentry's teatime to five o'clock when it has always been four o'clock. Well, that caused all sorts of trouble. Mr Cooper had to rewrite all the schedules, so he did.'

'Really? I had no idea servants had schedules.'

'Ay, it's back-breaking work, so it is, and no-one never knows the hardships we poor mugs have to endure. Downtrodden, we are. Even on Christmas Eve, Mr Cooper was running around like a headless chicken, he were. I had to ring the gong. Never had to do that before.' He nodded for emphasis, leaning against the mantelpiece as though he were settling in for the day.

'Just a moment! Are you telling me that it wasn't Cooper who rang the gong on Christmas Eve?'

'No, I did it, and it's not my job, you know. Not right, it ain't, there's trade unions nowadays, and they says –'

'Cartwright, just shut up a moment, will you?' That had set my mind running. Cooper wasn't even on my list of suspects, although he had reason enough to shoot the woman – she had threatened to put him out to pasture, and there was no pasture. 'Where was he?' was the obvious next question.

'Said to me the Christmas punch weren't right and told me to bang the gong. He went off to the kitchen to get more nutmeg, but when he came back it were without the nutmeg anyway. Then all hell broke loose upstairs and I thought no more about it – the nutmeg and the punch, that is.'

'Was His Lordship in the hall when Cooper left?'

'Certainly was, but he didn't take much notice, just kept staring up at the staircase waiting for folk to come down.'

A question flashed into my mind. 'Do any of the servants wear hair oil, to your knowledge?'

'They do not. Mr Cooper has banned it, so he has. Greasy, he says, gets on the uniforms and the furniture and is a devil to get rid of. So no one's allowed to wear it. Except him, of course. He wears it, which ain't right neither. There's a word for that, there is.'

'Hypocrite, I think you mean.' Irritating as Cartwright was, this conversation was proving most enlightening.

'Can't say I'd noticed any hair oil on Cooper. Are you sure about this, Cartwright?'

'I am, 'cause I can smell it. Got a rare nose, I have.'

'Indeed you have.' It was impossible not to notice his huge conk every time one had the misfortune to encounter him. 'Right, off you go,' I told him, 'haven't got time to waste in chit-chat.'

'Well, if you haven't, just you think about how much work I'm doing round here. Up and down stairs all day long –'

'Out!' I got up and held the door open, and he went off muttering about haystacks and the nobs getting their comeuppance.

Cooper had told me that he was in the vicinity of Cartwright for the whole of Christmas Eve, but now I'd discovered he was actually elsewhere at the very moment Sophia was shot.

My mind was churning with questions and trying to note them in my book had caused much scratching-out and a couple of ink blots. I may have to invest in another journal if this carries on.

As I trotted down the stairs looking for Cooper, I noticed the gnome-like figure of Tom standing before the hearth and staring around the hall with an awed expression in his eyes.

'Hello there, Tom,' I greeted him. 'Looking for me?'

'It's a big tree, ain't it.'

I regarded the drooping Christmas tree, busily dropping its needles in the corner of the hall. 'Indeed it is … did you come to discuss something – other than trees?'

'Ay, I did.'

'What was it?'

'Big room this, ain't it?'

'Yes. Um … Tom. What did you want to ask me?'

'I ain't been inside afore.'

'Right, well, now you have. Was there something you wanted to talk to me about?'

'That bloke what fell.'

'Yesterday – yes?'

'I think 'e had summat in his hand, but it got throwed as 'e tumbled down.'

I took a step back in surprise – that, and an attempt to distance myself from the pungent aroma emerging from Tom as his clothes began to dry out.

'Did you find it? Whatever it was?'

'No.'

'Did you search for it?'

'Ay, I did. This morning, soon as it were light. But it were all a mess, you know. The terrace, it were all rucked up after them blokes came an' shifted the gent what was dead to the butcher's store. Trampled all over, they did.'

'I'll come with you Tom, we'll have a look together.'

'As you say, Mr Major Lennox.'

I togged up against the treacherous outdoors, noticing that Tom was wearing clouted clogs with nails driven through, strapped to his boots, and I wished I had the same. I tied a couple of scarves around my footwear for traction and picked up my walking stick as we left the house.

He was right about the terrace: it looked treacherous. Peregrine's outline was still distinct, but everywhere else was churned up, with frozen mounds and icy holes made by heavy boots.

'We'll start with a square search, Tom. You take that side of the terrace, I'll do this one. Off you go.'

I'm not sure he understood what I meant by a square search, but he went off anyway and wandered about. After an hour in the bone-chilling cold we had failed to achieve anything other than possible frostbite.

'Tom, are you quite sure he threw something? Seems a bit pointless once one knows one's embarked on a terminal plummet.'

'It could 'ave been chucked by the murderer, to 'ide the foul deed as what 'e did, 'is 'eart filled with evil.' Tom said this with considerable drama by strangulating the final words and raising his hand as though fending off some fiendish killer. I was beginning to think he'd missed his calling – he'd have made a fine character actor should anyone be in need of a short, bandy-legged, toothless old man.

'If that were the case, it could be further away. What did you see exactly?'

'A shinin' sliver of light spinnin' in yonder air, fallin' to the deadenin' clod of earth like that bloke with wings what melted.'

'Yes, excellent, Tom. Very illuminating.' I picked my way slowly toward the low box hedge blanketed beneath a snowdrift at the border of the terrace. Tom's superior footwear enabled him to forge ahead of me and he let out a yell.

'I found it. It's a bottle, so it is.'

I rushed as quickly as I could without my feet going from under me. Tom was carefully wiping the bottle clean as I reached him.

'Fingerprints! No, Tom! Don't wipe off the prints!'

He turned to look at me in dismay, then dropped the bottle, which smashed on the icy step he was standing on.

'Oh, buggeration! You shouldn't a' yelled at me like that, Mr Major Lennox, look what you done now.'

'Oh hell.' I ran my fingers through my hair as I looked down at the shattered remains. 'Couldn't be helped, Tom – but please don't touch it, will you. Let me do it.'

He stood aside as I took out my jam jar and carefully filled it with shards of glass with the aid of my tweezers. Fingerprints were now out of the question. The bottle bore no label, but I knew what it had contained by the smell: it was hair oil.

I returned to the house, Cooper was still not in evidence. I questioned a footman, who told me he had no idea where the butler was to be found, which I thought was very strange, and there seemed to be some tension among the servants.

The bottle of hair oil occupied my thoughts. Why not take the item with them once Peregrine had been stuffed out of the window? Why toss it into the garden where it would eventually be discovered – if not by me then almost certainly by the Bill? It had been brought there specifically to smear the window – a clever trick by someone who had thought the whole process through, except for this. I mulled it over for some minutes, and then snapped to: Cooper was in my sights and I needed him to answer some very serious questions – like where the hell was he at the time?

My search turned up nothing in the house or kitchens, just a number of worried faces and shrugs. I returned to the hall and once more donned outdoor togs and headed for the door. Fogg had accompanied me on my peregrinations about the house, but now realised we were about to depart the warmth and shelter of the great indoors, and scarpered. My footsteps took me to the butchery and Mr Biggs, that being the region Cooper had been reported as heading towards when last heard of.

'Oh, it's you then.' Thud. Biggs was applying his cleaver to the bones of the latest fallen beast.

'Indeed it is!' I remarked. 'Have you seen Cooper?' Thud.

'Ay.' Thud.

'Where?' Thud.

'Out there.' Thud. Biggs paused to raise his bloodied chopper and pointed it toward a building with a door that stood half open, on the other side of the frozen courtyard.

'Thank you, Biggs.' I waited for the thud, but it didn't come.

'You doin' the detecting, ain't you?' He held the cleaver in his huge hand, blood trickling down its razor-sharp edge to drip onto the carcass he was butchering.

'Um, yes. Seems to be the general opinion, anyway.'

'Like what they do in books, then?'

'Yes. You don't happen to know Tom from the garden, do you?' I enquired.

'Ay, we be in the book club, 'im and me. We read out extracts by lamplight in our 'umble 'ovels, we do, gathered aroun' the burnin' 'arth.'

'Really? Fascinating.' Damn strange bunch of people employed amongst the outdoor staff. 'Do you live in humble hovels, then? Because if you do, I'll be having a word with His Lordship about it.'

'Well, they're not that 'umble – and nor be they 'ovels. I was tryin' to portray the illusion of simple men 'onourin' the majesty of the written word. That's all.' His face had taken on a slightly glazed look; now he lowered his cleaver and leaned toward me. 'I pretend I'm not 'ere and nor is all these dead animals. I like readin' poetry, like brave Lochinvar.' Biggs raised his arm and quoted: ''E staid not for brake, and 'e stopp'd not for stone. 'E swam the Eske River where ford weren't there none, But 'ere 'e alighted at Netherby gate, The bride 'ad consented, the gallant come late: For a laggard in love, and a dastard in war, Was to wed the fair Ellen of brave Lochinvar ...' The butcher dragged a blood-spattered sleeve across his eyes and picked up his axe again.

Thud.

'Right.' I pulled myself out of my transfixed state. 'I'll be off then.' Thud.

'Ay.' Thud.

I crossed the frozen expanse of cobbled yard slightly bemused. I must say I had uncovered all sorts of fascinating facts, like servants come in many different varieties and veins but underneath it all they're just like us really.

The store with the half-open door was carpeted with a thick layer of straw. In one corner lay the earthly remains of Peregrine Kingsley, looking quite blue and rather ghastly. Someone had taken the time to close his eyes and mouth and fold his arms neatly across his chest. In life he would have been quite comfortable in a straw nest such as this, though I doubt he'd have appreciated it.

In the other corner of the room Cooper sat propped against the wall: eyes tight shut, mouth agape, and looking almost as dreadful as yesterday's corpse.

CHAPTER 18

I approached with difficulty; the straw was knee-deep and I virtually had to wade through it.

'Cooper?' I called, but received no response.

I ploughed on and reached his side to give him a prod. 'Cooper?'

He let out a loud snore – well at least he wasn't dead. And now that I was next to him I could smell the reason for his comatose state: brandy. Down in the depths of straw I noticed a glint of metal. I pulled it out – it was a silver hip flask engraved with fancy lettering, 'P.B.K.', better known as Peregrine Bertram Kingsley. I gave it a quick shake – it was empty.

'Cooper.' I prodded him again, then shook him, making the straw rustle and causing dust to drift up. I let go of his lapels and sneezed, which did the trick, as his eyes suddenly flew open.

'Sir!' he uttered in horror.

'What are you doing, Cooper?'

He let out a loud groan, then stood up sharply and started brushing straw from his clothes with frantic hands. The damn stuff had got itself everywhere and I helped flick it off his back, but he remained dishevelled even after our best efforts.

'Sir.' He couldn't look me in the eye, preferring to direct his speech at my boots. 'Sir,' he began again.

'Yes, yes, I'm still here. What caused you to binge on the brandy, Cooper?'

'An unfortunate incident, sir, though it is no excuse for my appalling lapse. I must go and offer my resignation to His Lordship immediately.'

He proceeded to wade toward the door, raising more dust as he went.

I sneezed again, then stopped him. 'Nonsense! We would be lost without you. Just tell me what the devil's going on.'

'Laundry-maid – Doris,' he muttered.

I concluded that Doris was the object of a romantic fancy and the resultant wooing had not gone well.

'Yes?'

'I harboured hopes, sir, that we would wed. But it is not to be.' He straightened his back, pulling himself together.

'Ah, well, I commiserate, Cooper. Ladies can be fickle, you know, often observed it myself. Complete mystery most of the time.'

'Yes, sir, as you say, sir.'

'Doris wasn't by any chance the reason you didn't ring the gong, was she? I mean the night the Countess was shot?'

'She was, sir. I had a small gift prepared for her; I wanted to deliver it in person.'

'Right. Good explanation. Excellent.'

Must say I was very relieved to hear it. Having done all this detecting work just to uncover Cooper's culpability and have him hanged would not have gladdened my heart one iota. Quite the reverse, in fact.

'Don't happen to know where you were at three o'clock yesterday, do you, Cooper?'

'Yes, sir, I was proposing to Doris, sir. On one knee, in the traditional manner.'

'Quite. That's the way it should be done. I assume the answer was in the negative then?'

'She asked for time to reflect, sir. And then this morning she informed me she was unable to accept my offer, as she had formed an attachment elsewhere.'

'Good Lord. Who is it?'

'Cartwright, sir. They are to be wed and have formed a plan to move to Bridlington and open a tea shop.'

'Capital! Can't stand the man.' I glanced at Cooper's face, noticed the manly tremor that passed across his lips, and hastily back-tracked. 'Um, I mean, terrible lapse of judgement on the part of Doris ... but Bridlington is a long way off and it will allow you to bear the parting more easily. And as for Cartwright – further away the better, in my view.'

'As you say, sir.'

'Right,' I decided, 'better get on.' I tossed the flask in Kingsley's direction as we departed, locked the door behind us and left him in solitary interment.

Cooper trudged off to brush himself down, take a couple of powders and get back to it. As indeed I was itching to do, so I retired to my rooms to note down the day's endeavours and ponder my next moves.

The dinner gong sounded as I was writing. I was dashed hungry, and with Fogg in tow I entered the dining room to find a complete ensemble of the family.

'Greetings, Uncle, Edgar, all and sundry!'

Uncle beamed hazily – looked like he'd started on the port way ahead of me – but I couldn't get a peep from the others. Natasha was already in place. I stopped short when I noticed Gertrude, who was festooned in a heavy black veil so dense that it may not even have been her underneath it.

'I'm sorry about your loss, Gertrude,' I offered by way of a salute. I waited for some sort of response but nothing came: she retained her usual mantis-like pose, clutching her handbag tightly.

'We were holding a minute's silence in memory of Peregrine,' Edgar said sharply.

'Well, I wish you'd mentioned that before!'

He ignored me. 'We'll have to start again now.'

He placed his watch back on the table in front of him; I could hear the tick in the silence as I bowed my head, before I gave a mighty sneeze.

'Sorry, sorry, damn straw gets right up the nose.'

A metallic crash sounded behind me and I swung round to see that Cooper had dropped a whole ham in a covered serving dish. Footmen scrambled to clean up, and the butler left the room with his face red and looking more than a trifle out of sorts.

'Right, let's try that again, shall we?' Edgar glared at his watch, and we all bowed our heads once more.

Adam had dressed entirely in mourning gear, black everything apart from his white shirt – he looked as if he were auditioning for a bloody minstrel show. How did they know to pack mourning clothes? Or do people always travel with them on the off chance that someone's going to drop off the twig? Then again, maybe they did it and came prepared?

Finally, we started on the soup and I tucked in. Gertrude, of course, was flummoxed because she either had to remove the ridiculous get-up she was wearing or stay hungry. I could see her knuckles whitening around the handle of her bag.

'Gertrude, can I help?' I offered.

Nothing, not a flicker; and her soup would soon be stone cold. Adam was talking animatedly to Uncle and wasn't even looking, so I picked up her spoon and dangled it over her soup dish, threatening to drop it in. She threw back the veil and snatched it off me.

'Don't.' She glared at me. 'It will make a mess, you know I hate mess,' she hissed.

She ate in silence without giving me any thanks for solving her dilemma.

Chatter was subdued given that Peregrine's demise had only happened yesterday. I held off asking anyone where they'd been at the time as it probably would have seemed insensitive. Adam piped up just as pudding was being dished out.

'As I was telling you earlier, Lord Melrose, reducing staffing levels and expanding the amount of land under cultivation to include some of the lawns along the drive would be pretty much all you'd need to do to bring this place back into profit.'

Uncle stared at him through unfocused eyes, swaying slightly in his seat.

'Adam.' I felt a sudden surge of anger. I stood up and bellowed at him.

'You are not going to have any influence in this house whatsoever. Not today, not next year, not ever! You keep your sticky fingers a long way from my uncle and Melrose Court, or I'll have your bloody hide and nail it to the front door as a warning to all thieves and charlatans of your ilk.'

Silence prevailed for a frozen moment until Uncle broke into laughter, followed by Edgar – although I'm still not sure why they thought it was funny.

Adam raised his hands in a calming motion. 'Now come along, Lennox, old boy, it was just a suggestion, you know. No need to get worked up about it.'

'Right, well keep your suggestions to yourself,' I snapped back. 'And I apologise for my language, ladies.'

I looked from one to the other. They both stared back with wide-eyed interest, almost admiration, as though I done something remarkable. And Gertrude didn't spring to her saintly husband's defence either.

The remainder of the meal passed quietly; people seemed to be tiptoeing around me, which I have to say got a tad annoying after a while; so rather than go through the formalities with the port I shoved off for an early night.

The next morning I woke bright and early to the realisation that my breath was no longer visible. I opened the curtains to a thin sun in a clear sky – a thaw was setting in. How long would I have before Chief Inspector Swift and the constabulary were able to get through? I pushed the window open and leaned out. Snow and ice were still thick upon the ground, but puddles of water were forming and icicles were dripping from the ledges. Today would be my last day of peaceful investigation. Tomorrow the roads would be open.

I sighed, closed the window, jollied the fire to life and reached for my notebook and pen. At the top of a virgin page I wrote: 'Adam?' And underneath it, I entered: 'Edgar?'

Cooper arrived with breakfast before I could make any further progress.

'How goes it?' I asked him as he set down my favourite meal on my cluttered desk beside the fire.

'Very well, sir.'

'I mean, is all well with you, Cooper?' I think he was avoiding the subject of yesterday's contretemps.

'Indeed it is, sir.'

'Cartwright formed any plans to depart yet?'

'I believe he has handed in his notice, sir. His and his fiancée's departure is set for New Year's Day.'

'Excellent, sooner the better.'

His face fell and shoulders slumped.

I tucked into bacon, eggs and fried bread thanking heavens Cook wasn't involved in the crisis.

Poor Cooper left with an air of despondency and Fogg and I completed breakfast, bath and toilette. Despite the urgency of my need to interview Adam and Edgar, the lure of the woods got the better of me and I took off for a soggy tramp through silent pathways among trees dripping with melting snow. We turned to walk around a fallen log and came across a fox with a cock pheasant in its jaws. The fox's coat gleamed red in the weak sun as it paused to look at us. Fogg froze as I shifted my shotgun to my shoulder, I watched it, it watched me, then I let it go on its way. It was a scrawny vixen in need of food and I hadn't the heart to shoot her. After all, she'd done no more than survival dictated.

'Blanket.' Fogg was taken off to dry as was our routine and I returned to my rooms to collect notebook and pen and wandered down to meet Adam in the drawing room, where I'd left orders for him to await me.

'Adam.'

'Lennox.'

He was still dressed in mourning garb – trying too damn hard for sympathy, in my book. I was in no mood for sentiment, real or feigned.

'You're taking this a bit far, old man,' Adam complained. 'The police are the chaps to deal with this. You have no right to go around questioning people.'

'I don't need the "right", I'm doing it and you'll bloody well cooperate,' I snapped back.

He frowned, and then glared into the fire, watching the flames, his face as sulky as a recalcitrant schoolboy's.

'Really, I don't know what's come over you, Lennox.'

Ignoring his whining, I flicked through my notebook to my list of questions.

'When did the Countess approach you and your father to draw up the new will disinheriting Edgar and me?'

'Oh, is this what it's about? You're sore! Well, let me tell you, old man, we were only doing as instructed, and believe me, it would have been worse if we hadn't tried to rein her in. I know you don't think so, but we were doing you and Edgar a lot of favours with that. You could have tied her up in litigation for years simply because of the way we'd drafted it.'

'Cut it out, Adam, and tell me the date.'

He sniffed and crossed his arms.

'Early in December, about three weeks before it was due to be signed.'

'Which was to be on Christmas Eve.' I noted the dates down. 'Where did this take place – here, or in London?'

'London.'

'Edgar's apartment in Eaton Square?'

He nodded and crossed his legs – he was going to tie himself in knots if he carried on.

'Wonderful way for the Countess to repay Edgar's generosity,' I commented dryly. 'Was Natasha present?'

'No, she had nothing to do with it. I doubt she even knew about it.'

'Yet she and Peregrine had been lovers.'

His eyebrows shot up. 'How did you know that?'

I ignored his question; I had enough of my own to ask. 'When did he start the relationship?'

'I say, Lennox, this is rather infra dig!'

'Adam,' I said firmly.

'Very well. Earlier this year, I don't know when exactly. You know my Papa, Lennox, always had some fruity piece on his arm. They came and went, never took much notice, really.'

'Do you think this was different?'

'I suppose she was different. Much more a serious contender than his usual type. High-stepper, you know. Class bred into her blood and bones – and it shows.'

'Would the relationship have come off if she hadn't met Edgar?'

'I doubt it, given the age gap – but she never entirely let Papa go. Strung him along even after she'd moved into Edgar's apartment with her aunt.'

'Did she have a use for him? Legally, I mean. She and Sophia would be in need of help, one way or another.'

'I think there may have been something. I'd have to go through his papers to find out. Are you thinking of anything in particular?'

'Where are they, these papers?'

'The most important ones would be in his briefcase. Must still be in his rooms I suppose, I haven't felt up to going in there yet.'

I went to the bell pull for attention and asked the attending footman to bring it. A few minutes later I tipped out its contents on the coffee table.

'Lennox, I protest! Some of this stuff is confidential.' Adam stood up to object.

I ignored him and started to place the papers in piles between items pertaining to Uncle's affairs and others'. I soon discovered there was very little in the way of others'. Despite Peregrine's assertions that he was an expert adviser to many clients, it was obvious he was not. There were carbon copies of correspondence between him and Natasha and a couple of pithy letters from a very angry client, and that was pretty much it.

'Who is Sir Jasper Laycock?'

'Ah – that would be Gertrude's father.'

'Really.' I raised my eyebrows as I read the terse notes. 'Interesting choice of wording, very colourful!'

'I think he became a little overexcited. He'll calm down, they usually do.'

I laid the letters between Peregrine and Natasha aside, which were all formal client–lawyer types about gaining necessary certificates for residence in this country. It wasn't just the contents that interested me but the style. I stuffed the rest back into the briefcase, locked it, pocketed the key and parked it at my side. I had no intention of giving it back.

'Do you recall making fireworks when we youngsters?'

Adam looked at me as if I'd lost my marbles. 'Umm, not really. What are you getting at?'

'We used to make our own fireworks, remember? Like toffee apples: dunking them in wax to slow the bang so we could make a big show around the bonfire.'

'You mean you and Edgar did. You never let me join in anything. Used to call me Adam Snot.' He adopted a schoolboy tone: 'Adam snot allowed because he has to keep his clothes clean. Adam snot coming because his Pa won't let him get covered in hay. Adam snot included because he doesn't play with the local boys.'

I laughed, then noticed his expression and stopped. 'I'd forgotten about that. No point it getting annoyed about it now, Adam, you know what dreadful little oiks schoolboys can be.'

'Scarred me for life, that did.'

'War scars you for life, Adam. Childhood prepares you for it. What did you do during the war? Remind me again.'

'You know what I did, Lennox.'

'Royal Defence Corps wasn't it? Spent your time guarding Brighton Pier?'

'And other places! It's not my fault I have flat feet.'

'There was the Medical Corps.'

'I faint at the sight of blood.'

That was a lie too, but I let it pass.

'Did you ever handle munitions or detonators?'

'Good God, no! Gertrude knows more about that sort of thing than I do. Practically sat on her father's lap as he manufactured bombs.'

I wasn't getting any closer to pinning him down; he'd always been adept at snaking his way around awkward questions.

I changed tack. 'Your father lied to me.'

'When?'

'Frequently! But most specifically about where he was at five forty-five on Christmas Eve. The time at which the Countess was shot.'

'He was with me. We were having a drink in my suite.'

'I know you weren't.'

'How do you know?'

'Gertrude told me. And she doesn't lie.'

'In his rooms, then.' Adam scowled at me.

'You don't have an alibi.' I jotted that down in my notebook. 'Where were you when your father fell to his death?'

'Look, Lennox, this is too much. He may not have been much of a father, but you can't go round accusing me of doing him in.'

'Just answer the damn question, Adam.'

'I was with Gertrude – ask her. As you said, she doesn't lie.'

With that, he got up and walked out, a big grin spreading across his face.

CHAPTER 19

The lunch gong sounded but I ignored it, having better things to do, such as putting my thoughts in order. Despite his evasions, Adam had given me the clue I needed. Preparing for the interview with Edgar was going to be more tricky; plus the very idea gave me a heavy heart.

I retreated to the window seat of my rooms and watched the activity below; I imagined Mr Biggs chopping away at some carcass, and Tom out there somewhere, his mind on whatever book he had in his pocket. I watched the laundry maids dashing back and forth, and wondered which of them was Doris. Should I double check with her, that she and Cooper truly were together on the occasions of each murder? No – I dismissed the idea – Cooper didn't do it. I knew who it was, and I was reasonably certain I could prove it, but there were still a couple of mysteries that I wanted to solve first.

I was restless. It wasn't so much that I couldn't cudgel my thoughts into order than that I didn't really want to. I trotted downstairs to the kitchens and helped myself to a large slice of game pie to share with Fogg, who was still in his cosy basket next to the stove. I sat quietly amongst the hustle and bustle of maids stirring pots, cooks making pastry, others up to their elbows in suds washing piles of dishes.

My mind wandered to the subject of legs. Ladies' legs, actually, which had always drawn my interest. As a child I'd become curious as to whether ladies actually had legs – it was hard to tell as they glided about in their floor-length frocks. At around the age of five or six I decided to find out for myself by lifting one of the nursery maids' skirts to have a look – that got me my first real spanking, which I consider grossly unfair to this day. Since then ladies' hemlines have risen, from floor to ankle to calf and now to the knee (a fashion I for one heartily endorse, particularly as silk stockings have flourished as a consequence). Such gentle musing sent me off in a lighter mood for an interview I had been dreading: my meeting with Edgar.

He was seated in the library reading a book, feet up on a stool in front of a blazing fire, as we were all wont to do in the depths of winter.

'Lennox,' he greeted me, barely glancing up from the page.

'Questions, old boy.'

'What?'

'Need to ask you some questions, Edgar.'

He realised from my tone that this wasn't a casual visit and placed a marker in his page, closed the book and put it aside.

'Fire away, Lennox. Pleased to hear you're taking this new career seriously.'

I sat down opposite, crossed my legs and opened my notebook. Edgar smiled when he saw my actions, but held his tongue.

'What do you know about wax?'

That brought a frown to his face. 'What sort of wax?' he asked. 'Carnauba, bees', paraffin, shellac, sealing wax? Or are you talking about the wax from the fireplace?'

'Yes I am. Do you remember those fireworks we made when we were children?'

'Oh, the delayed-action bangers we used to place around the bonfire to make a firework display – yes, I do. Do you think that's how the noise was made, the bang we heard after Sophia was killed?'

'Yes.'

He rubbed his chin. 'Ha! Simple but effective. Very good – and well done for working it out. They stank, though, didn't they? There were chicken feathers in the wax, and burned feathers always stink. Who got the wax for us? Can't remember his name? It was that young lad who was boot-boy. Killed in 1914 almost as soon as he got off the boat, poor blighter.'

Edgar was right, the butchery wax stank when burned, I'd forgotten that very relevant point. I jotted it down in my notebook before answering.

'Ned Potter. Joined up before anyone could stop him; he was only fifteen but told them he was older. Damn shame, actually, he was a bright spark.'

The memories caused us a moment's pause, and then we eyed each other warily.

'Is that all, Lennox? Because I was enjoying my book before you came in.'

'I wish it were,' I said, and meant it. 'Any idea where you were when the Countess was shot?'

'What time did you say she was killed?'

'Five forty-five, just as the gong sounded for the gift-giving.'

'Do you actually know that for a fact?'

I told him about the watch and its simple malfunction that fixed the time of death. I think he was quietly impressed.

'Very well ... Yes ... I was collecting my things together in my rooms, preparing to come downstairs. Where were you?'

'Doing the same.'

'Doesn't help either of us, does it?'

'It's irrelevant, Edgar. A murderer has to have a good reason to kill because they're putting their life on the line too.'

'Are you saying I had cause to kill the Countess?'

'She wasn't a countess. But you knew that, didn't you?'

He smiled briefly and nodded. His expression was one I didn't see too often: cold, calculating, distant – the real Edgar beneath the veneer.

'Sophia loaned you money and you couldn't pay it back.'

'How did you find out about that?'

'I didn't, but it was the only conclusion that made sense. You set me on this trail, Edgar. Use my erratic mind, you said.'

'Ha! Hoist by my own petard. Yes, more fool me, well done, Lennox.'

'So, when Sophia lent you the money, did she blackmail you into romancing Natasha?'

'No, nothing at all to do with it.' He shook his head emphatically.

'But you were her entrée into society? And her introduction to Uncle?'

'I was, but I wasn't her sole supporter. Peregrine had been close to them before me.'

'Once Sophia lent you money and you were unable to pay her back, she became short of cash herself, didn't she?

He didn't reply, just watched me with a cold expression.

'Is that when she started using fake bank drafts to buy jewellery?'

'Perhaps,' Edgar replied. 'I don't know. I intended to repay her, and I would have done, in time. But she was an impetuous woman and she liked to deck herself out in baubles. It really was quite ridiculous, but I suppose she was desperate to become the de facto noble lady she was pretending to be.'

'Natasha said Sophia panicked when people began to talk about the frauds and started to repay them. Where did she get the money?'

'I have no idea ... It wasn't from me.' His eyes darkened as he stared at me; these were secrets he had never wanted to discuss. I'm sure he felt ashamed of them, but it was his own damn fault.

'Peregrine? Do you think he lent it to her? Or Adam?'

'Probably not Adam, he's mostly a false front. So was Peregrine, but he could lay his hands on money when he had to.'

'Were you in debt to him, too?' I asked.

'No. I'd had enough dealings with Peregrine in the past to know the stupidity of taking that track. He was a thief that preyed on whoever he could con.'

'Wish you'd informed me. I always suspected him – loathed him, actually, but never had any real evidence that he was a crook.'

Edgar shrugged. 'I warned you, wasn't that enough?'

'Touché,' I replied. 'I told you that Sophia had bought the necklace from me with a fraudulent draft.'

'Yes, Lennox. Nothing wrong with my memory, old man.'

'Did you know that she was committing fraud prior to my telling you?'

'No, but I suspected it when I saw the damn thing hanging around her neck.'

'When was that?'

'About a week or so before she and Natasha arrived here. Around the beginning of December. I don't know how long she'd had it. I'd been away for months on the Continent, and had come back briefly to see 'Tasha and pick up some new clothes before I headed back to France. Then finally I returned and headed straight down here, arriving on the same day as you. The girls had already been here about ten days at Uncle's invitation.'

'Did you tell Natasha about your suspicions?'

'Eventually, yes, I did mention it.'

'When?'

'When I dropped in for my new suit.'

I wrote the dates down. Natasha probably warned Sophia around the same time and that set the ball rolling for the fat man to arrive at my door.

'Who was the fat man, Edgar? He had to be associated with your place in Eaton Square, there's no other way Sophia could have met him. She couldn't roam the streets of London looking for someone to make these transactions for her.'

'Remind me again what he looked like.'

'Hugely overweight. Boxer, I think – ex-boxer, anyway – he had the nose and ears for it. But he'd run to fat, as though his fighting days were done and he no longer had to keep fit.'

Edgar picked his book up again, turning it over in his hands, his mind revolving with it. 'The coal man – forgive my vagueness, but I don't spend much time with tradesmen. I think it may have been Porkie Pye – his actual name is George Pye – a Belgravia coal merchant. I've only met the man in passing, usually when he's shoving his overdue bill under my nose.'

That made sense: Porkie was the name on Sophia's telegram, although I wasn't ready to share that information with Edgar. I felt somewhat deflated and upset at the extent of the deceit around me. And that the closest person I had to a brother in the world was part of the mesh of lies.

'I'm sorry, Lennox. I should have told you.' Edgar smiled quietly. 'It was a bit of a joke at first, setting you off on the track of a murderer – rather a black joke, in hindsight. But I needed some space to work out what was going on and what to do about it. I think it's all rather backfired on me, hasn't it?'

'Not just you, Edgar. Two people are dead and someone's going to hang for it.'

'Would you like a drink, Lennox?'

'Yes, I think I would.'

He went to the tantalus and opened the brandy decanter, poured us each a snifter and handed one to me. We drank in silence, our thoughts consuming us.

'What are you going to do?' he asked me.

'Telephone Swift. He'll be here in the morning and there are a few items I need him to bring with him.'

'Lennox, I can't ask you to overlook the incident, can I? Just turn the other cheek, as it were? I promise you there won't be a repetition.'

'No, Edgar, I can't. Once someone uses murder as a solution, it's too tempting to apply that same solution to other problems. I will not let a murderer off the hook.'

I finished my drink and left him where I'd found him.

The telephone in the hall lacked privacy: almost anyone passing or lurking around could overhear a conversation. But there was another set of apparatus at the gatehouse and I felt in need of fresh air and a stretch of the legs. I found my dog, ordered him from his comfortable nest and made him accompany me on a long walk down the slush-covered drive to the front gates.

I made my telephone call to the bemusement of the lodge-keeper. It was a long conversation. Swift was disinclined to believe a word at first – seemed he still thought I was the most likely suspect; but after the details about the watch and the various incidents, he began to listen more attentively. By the time I finished he had agreed to my requests, although he retained a dubious tone to the end.

I warned Trent, the gateman, not to repeat a word and he nodded dumbly in acquiescence. Then I wended my way slowly back to the house with my dog at my heels and my mind deep in thought – thoughts of wax, actually, and the unravelling of puzzles.

CHAPTER 20

I skipped dinner, relaying my apologies via Cooper, and took off like a sneak to poke around my prime suspect's rooms. Should I ever again carry out any detecting, I'd rather not be obliged to act like a thief in the night.

Despite my dislike of the clandestine act, I did find what I was looking for, and carried it off with a lighter step. I had assembled as much evidence as I could, and was now keen to set it all up and make sense of it.

I returned to my rooms, and after Cooper had served my dinner on a tray, I sought to arrange things in intelligible order. The Old Bill would arrive on the morrow and I had to be ready. The most vital piece of evidence was the Countess's old watch and I placed this to the top left of my desk upon a single page of notes that I hoped would make clear its full import.

Next was the jar of wax from Mr Biggs the butcher. This was a negative piece of evidence designed to prove that it was not the source of paraffin wax because of the feathers and smelly detritus it encased.

I added a note about the M-80 firecracker. Swift had

categorically refused to bring an M-80, as he considered them far too dangerous, despite my pleading.

It would have been useful to place my little pocket pistol alongside the note, but as the police had confiscated it I had to trust Inspector Swift to bring it with him. Thankfully he had agreed to that one, but had made a fuss about ammunition and I had to swear I didn't have any hidden anywhere.

The jar with the charred remains of the telegram was next, underpinned by a brief note regarding Edgar's address, and the source of information (being the loquacious and irritating Cartwright).

My jar of broken shards that had been the bottle of hair oil belonged to the top right of the desk. This was my section for Peregrine's demise. Actually, it was all I had for his death, as defenestration was a straightforward means of murder without much in the way of paraphernalia.

The filched item I'd stolen this evening I now set down on the left, which was the Countess's side of the equation. In the centre I arranged the bundle of papers I'd hijacked from Peregrine's briefcase, and next to them I added my concisely written notes. On top of that I placed my mother's ruby necklace, which gave me pause, as I was loath to see it in such a context.

It occurred to me that my collection was looking a little sparse. Should I reconstruct a toffee-apple firecracker? Would the police know what I was talking about when I explained delayed-action bangers? Actually, they almost certainly would because most of them had just fought a war and things going boom were an all too familiar experience.

And so early to bed and wake up fresh for tomorrow's piece of theatre.

The police arrived at first light, earlier than expected. Swift had moved speedily and Cooper, bearing my breakfast tray, gave me the news that even now they were scouring the grounds, the east terrace, the third-floor corridor and the butcher's store.

I was barely dressed and shaved when a rap came on my door. I opened it to admit Inspector Swift himself.

'So, you think you have the murders solved?' he asked, eyeing me in that mordant way he had, shoulders slightly hunched, leaning forward like a hawk who'd spotted a particularly tasty little shrew.

'Yes,' I responded calmly. 'Sit down.'

He placed himself at the desk, where I had arranged the evidence. As I talked him through each piece he scrutinised the items, picking them up to examine them. I explained the relevance of each and the sequence of events, and concluded with the name of the murderer.

By this time his scepticism had abated, and he looked at me silently before withdrawing from his pocket the items he'd agreed to bring. He laid them carefully at the centre of the desk, below Peregrine's documents and the notes I had made.

'You've obviously spent a considerable amount of time on this, Major Lennox. You are intimately acquainted with these people and this house. This milieu is your environment – but let me explain something to you.' The Inspector came to face me where I was leaning against the window-seat. 'People who kill are dangerous. We are experienced in this: it is our investigation and it will be our arrest. I will accept your assistance because I am inclined to be persuaded by your findings. But you must give me your word now, before we go any further, that you will not try to run the show, because I'll damn well have you in gaol for obstruction if you do.'

'You have my word, Swift. I'm more than willing to let you and your men form the guard and arrest the killer, but you need to allow me to reveal the identity of the person responsible. Everyone involved must see the murderer's reaction. Everyone must observe and be convinced of the murderer's guilt, otherwise making your conviction stick will be obstructed and possibly fail. We may seem like a remnant of history, but our name still means something, even in this age of democracy. Do you understand me?' I asked.

Swift regarded me, eyes narrowed, mind patently ticking over; then he nodded sharply. 'Very well. What do you intend?'

I told him how I would construct the scene that would bring the name of the murderer into the open. Swift hesitated momentarily, then agreed.

As we prepared to leave, the Inspector withdrew from his pocket an object wrapped in a clean white cloth and laid it on my desk below the other items. It was a silver letter-opener in the shape of a dagger.

'Do you recognise it?' he asked.

'I have never laid eyes on it, but I heard Peregrine Kingsley refer to it. He said it was missing. Where did you find it?'

'On the east terrace. We brushed the stones free of the remaining slush and it was there, where his body had fallen. Must have been forced into the snow by his weight.'

'Did you find any fingerprints?

'No. The melting ice would have cleansed it.'

'May I add it to the evidence?'

'Yes, and you can use it in your Punch and Judy show if you wish,' he added dryly.

I ignored the remark and placed the letter-opener with the other evidence in a wooden box which I'd asked Cooper to furnish. We walked down to the drawing room together in silence.

A policeman in uniform stood outside the double doors and swung one open as we approached, then closed it with a click behind us. Each window and door was guarded by a constable. In the centre of the room, gathered in a semicircle, were members of the family. I had given explicit instructions as to where each must sit and everyone was already in their place. Swift and I proceeded to the fireplace and he stood to one side of the hearth as I removed my cache of exhibits and laid them out on the coffee table.

There was some murmuring, but I think they'd all expected some sort of police action today, and no significant protest was forthcoming.

'Good morning,' I began, then cleared my throat as they all turned to stare at me – I have to admit I felt a sudden shiver of nervousness, being at the centre of such a strange little drama.

'Don't drag it out, Lennox, will you, old boy,' Edgar said.

'Bit of patience required, I'm afraid,' I replied. 'I have a story to tell and you must all listen until it is concluded.' I looked around. Cooper was standing behind Uncle, who was seated nearest to me in his favourite wing chair. He was watching me, bushy eyebrows raised, slightly bemused but with an air of expectation. Edgar was next to him, dressed in a formal suit rather than country tweeds, I couldn't fathom why. Natasha was closest to him, seated within hand-holding distance. She wore the same dusky-rose silk frock she'd had on the night before Sophia died, and held an exquisitely embroidered deep-red velvet sac on her lap. It was the only time I'd ever seen her with any sort of bag. Back home in Russia she would have always had a maid or flunkey to carry her requisites. Maybe she was adjusting to our self-reliant provincial ways?

Adam and Gertrude shared a sofa. She was dressed in a shapeless mouse-brown gown and clutching her hand-bag as usual; he was still in his minstrel's mourning garb. Gertrude watched me with her habitual blank expression, while Adam stared around keen-eyed, no doubt wondering if there were any opportunities to off-load an extraneous watch or some such.

I cleared my throat and they all turned to face me.

'A little over a week ago a man died on the doorstep of my home in Ashton Steeple,' I began. 'At the time I had no idea who he was, why he was there or what he had died from, but his unfortunate demise has been followed by the deaths of two more people and an accusation that could have led to my facing the hangman. The local doctor, an old friend by the name of Cyril Fletcher, quickly discovered the cause of death to be a heart attack brought on by the man's excessive weight. That act of random misfortune toppled a stack of lies and deceit that has led us here today.'

I paused for a moment, looking at each of them, their eyes upon me but hiding their thoughts in expressions of neutral politeness. 'The fat man's name was George Pye, colloquially known as Porkie Pye. He was an ex-boxer and had become a coal merchant after giving up the ring. He was recruited by the woman we knew as Countess Sophia. She met him while staying at Edgar's house in Eaton Square. We know this because we have a telegram written by the "Countess" directed to George Pye.'

I held up the jar of blackened paper, which was met by blank incredulity by the assembled. I hastened on. 'The reason Sophia had enlisted the help of George Pye was that the task she had for him required someone with a dishonest nature.'

'If he was dead, how do you know?' Adam asked.

'Because the transactions he and the Countess dealt in were fraudulent,' I told him.

This caused a few eyebrows to raise. 'The Countess had a keen eye for expensive jewellery but lacked the means to pay for such things. To Sophia's mind, this was of little import. She had lived in a country where the ruling class could get away with anything, including murder. Defrauding 'little people' was minor in comparison.'

I paused to hold up the necklace.

'Where did you find that? It was missing from the Countess's body the night she was shot,' Gertrude snapped. She had a mind for this sort of detail.

'I was given it, wrapped up as a Christmas present. Someone's idea of a joke, I assume,' I answered tartly. 'As I was saying, when Sophia purchased my mother's ruby necklace, she was unaware that it was owned by a member of the gentry. She purchased it through a rather dubious acquaintance of mine, Frederick Hopper, simply thinking it belonged to a Major Lennox. She purchased her items herself, but she used George Pye to provide the fake bank drafts. Isn't that right, Inspector?'

I stood back a step to let him be more easily seen, as he was standing almost behind me.

'It is. I had it confirmed yesterday after you had provided me with his name and locale,' Swift stated.

I recommended, 'Uncle always referred to me as Heathcliff, so Sophia didn't make the connection until the evening we all had dinner together.'

'She was a pretty dubious character herself. She was not a countess, nor even a gentlewoman; she was, in fact, a servant, a nanny to a true noblewoman, Natasha Czerina Orlakov-Palen.'

'No!' Gertrude stood up, an expression of shock on her face. 'You mean she was a commoner? She lied to us? Adam, you should not be here to hear this tale of deception. We must leave.'

Adam waved his hands ineffectually at her. 'Now don't worry, old thing.'

Swift stepped forward. 'Sit down, madam. You and your husband will remain until I say you can go.'

She made to protest but two other policemen turned toward her, and she sank back onto her seat.

I was watching Uncle to see if the news came as a surprise to him. It didn't: he barely even blinked, just smiled vaguely at me, as though amused.

'Natasha was born into one of the highest families in Russia, and one of the most wealthy, were you not?' I turned to look at her and she gave a stiff nod of the head. 'An heiress to a colossal fortune, brought up to be the very epitome of nobility and utterly oblivious to the realities of the outside world. Until 1917, when all hell broke loose and your whole way of life came crashing around your ears. Everything you knew was utterly destroyed, as were your family; the only person you had left was your old nanny. Sophia had kept her wits; she gathered up your father's gold, and she used it to enable you both to flee the country. Paris must have been a relief to you, to be back amongst other Russian exiles, people of your own sort. But you were dismayed to see Sophia's desire to ape the aristocracy; she even began to style herself as a countess. Was her name actually Sophia, by the way? I know you said she had taken the identity of your real aunt.' I looked at Natasha, who stared icily back.

'It was, yes,' she replied coldly.

'Perhaps that's why she adopted the guise?' I asked. But the girl looked away, so I continued. 'It didn't work, did it: Sophia had no idea how to play the grand lady and you decided that London would make a better refuge, where there were fewer Russians. Somehow you made the acquaintance of Peregrine Kingsley – was that connection related to Sophia's need to exchange Russian gold for English pounds, perhaps?' I glanced at Natasha again, but she looked straight through me.

'Yes, it was,' Adam replied for her.

'And he made a killing from it,' Edgar snapped angrily.

Adam opened his mouth to argue, but I stepped in holding my hand up.

'Enough.' I turned back. 'Natasha, you began a relationship with Peregrine. I doubt you had any idea that he was short-changing Sophia. Your relationship with Kingsley eventually faltered, but fortuitously you and Edgar began to make a match of it. After the terrifying events you'd lived through, here, at last, was a ray of hope. A bright future with a wealthy young man who wanted to wed you. But Sophia's ambitions had run away with her and her arrogant disregard for the law was jeopardising that future. She was committing fraud. And she wasn't just defrauding saps like me, but people like Peregrine, and you, Adam.' I turned to face him as I finished the sentence.

'Don't drag me into this,' he said, his mouth tightening with fear.

'Sophia borrowed from you, didn't she? She had probably realised your father had taken advantage of her when exchanging the gold. She wouldn't have any compunction in visiting the same treatment on either of you. So she borrowed as much as you were willing to lend, no doubt at sky-high rates. Then she bought the stock your father had been so vigorously hawking in the Eastern Railway Company. I have to admit it was rather clever on her part; if the stocks did well she came out clutching a healthy profit; if they didn't do well,' I shrugged, 'then you and your father were the losers because she had no intention of paying you back.'

'How do you know all this?' Adam shouted at me.

'Because Major Lennox worked it out and asked me to check with the stock exchange and confirm it,' Swift interjected.

Edgar laughed, and so did Uncle.

'Sophia was such a bright lady. I'll never forget her,' Uncle said, half to himself.

'By this time Sophia had met Uncle Charles, so there was nothing Peregrine, or you, Adam, could do about her. You couldn't risk informing on her, or you'd lose the fees you and your father drew from this estate, and that was the only source of regular income you had. So you had to grin and bear it – but it must have been a bitter pill to swallow. And I don't imagine she would let you forget how you'd both tried to gull her.' I paused, and then went further. 'Nor were you and your father the only ones subject to her manipulations – were they, Edgar?' I turned to face him, and his expression darkened.

'Sophia loaned you money, then used it to keep you at her beck and call. She made you introduce her to the right people in society; people who she could use and possibly defraud. She was jeopardising your good name, and your career, wasn't she, Edgar?' I paused to look at him more closely. His expression had turned hard but he remained silent.

'She ran rings around the lot of us. Once she had secured her position as Lady Melrose, she would have held the reins entirely and used the whip as she felt fit. But one person couldn't accept that, and I cannot say I'm without sympathy. Poor Uncle may have thought Sophia was an exciting prospect, but she would have made our lives hell.'

I scanned my audience's faces; we were now approaching the meat of the matter and I had the undivided attention of the room. 'Sophia was shot using my pistol.' I picked it up, made a show of it, then placed it back down again. 'I think you all know that the time of her death was not in fact six o'clock when we all heard the bang, but was actually when the gong sounded, at five forty-five. We know the exact moment because that was when her watch stopped.' I held up the watch and their eyes followed my movements as though mesmerised.

'A strange piece; cheap, broken at the strap, and with an erratic mechanism. It gave me the clue to Sophia's identity because no countess would possess such a thing and certainly wouldn't display it if they did. The bang we heard was just that: a delayed-action firecracker, used as a subterfuge by the killer to confuse the time of death.'

'How was it done?' Gertrude interrupted. 'I am acquainted with ordinance, it's our family business.'

'Her father makes explosives,' Adam chipped in. 'Got a huge factory, he's worth a bomb!'

Swift eyed him closely, decided he was a harmless idiot and nodded to me to proceed. I explained at length the theft of the M-80 and the use of wax to delay it. Gertrude continued to question me, displaying an expert understanding of all things explosive. Had she not been wed to Adam, she might have made a perfect match for Lurch.

'What about the wax? You said it was paraffin wax, where was it from?' Gertrude demanded.

'At first I thought it was from the butchery here –' I briefly held up the jar of dingy wax '– but I concluded that it came from a different source. I will return to that later. Please be patient.'

I cleared my throat and Cooper kindly passed me a glass of water.

'The murderer wasn't content to merely confuse the time of death, they wanted to provide a culprit as well. So after shooting the Countess they ran up to my room by the back stairs and let Fogg loose, knowing he would

go and find me. That would force me to return with him
to my rooms. The murderer also knew I would have to
pass the drawing room – and their timing was perfect.
The plan was brilliant, and had it worked I would have
hanged. In one simple act, the murderer would have
removed the manipulative Sophia and the heir to both
the title and whatever is left of Uncle's fortune – wouldn't
he, Edgar?'

I turned now to focus on him. He glared at me.

'You needed money, Edgar.'

'You and I are quite aware of that, Lennox,' he replied.
'But I didn't need to kill for it.'

'No, you were going to marry Natasha and produce
the child who would unlock your own fortune. But
there was an impediment to this plan, and it was Peregrine who eventually brought it to your attention,
probably because he intended to blackmail you with it
at some time in the future. Natasha was already married.
Weren't you?' I moved to face her, watching a flush of
anger rise in her cheeks. 'You and Sophia escaped your
home near Moscow and fled to Petrograd and stayed
there. Why on earth would you remain in Russia after a
terrifying revolution that had led to the deaths of your
whole family? And why Petrograd, the scene of street
battles and bloody skirmishes between the remnants of
the White Russian Army and the Bolsheviks? The reason
was simple: your husband was there, Baron Ivanovich
Nikoli Palen. Baron Palen was head of one of the resistance groups fighting the Bolsheviks, and you stayed in

Petrograd until he was captured. And that is when you and Sophia fled to Paris.'

'He's dead, Lennox, how is this relevant?' Edgar asked.

'Because you were never sure that he was actually killed. I read the newspapers, just as we all do. I have a retentive mind for certain facts and I recall reading about that battle: it was brutal and ended in a massacre of the White Russian resistance. Baron Palen led one of the battalions and was reported missing; he had been taken prisoner by the Bolsheviks and very probably ended his days in the dungeons of Lubyanka Prison.'

'You have proof, I assume?' Edgar asked me.

I picked up the papers I'd taken from Peregrine's briefcase and read out an extract.

'The matter of the Palen certificate has now been resolved and it need no longer be of concern to you.' I replaced the papers and faced the girl. 'Natasha, this is a carbon copy of a letter addressed to you. I assume he was confirming that he had purchased a death certificate for your husband should the question of your children's legitimacy ever arise? But I contend the certificate was a fake. It is not possible to obtain certificates from Revolutionary Russia.' I looked back at her, and her expression was now of stone. I turned from her to face the other lady in the room.

'Gertrude, your father had been seriously duped by Peregrine, and he was very angry, wasn't he?'

She stared at me. 'Well? What of it?'

'And you really did loathe Peregrine, didn't you?' I went

on. He wanted to lock you away; he said you were mad. And you considered him debauched and a terrible influence on Adam.'

'He was evil, and God will now punish him. Peregrine will reap what he has sown,' Gertrude replied calmly.

'Did you help him get closer to God?'

A wicked grin touched her lips before she returned to her habitual, glassy-eyed stare. 'I prayed that both he and Sophia would be taken up as they deserved. Adam has convinced me that I am not the physical cause of their deaths. God will choose His own instruments. I have learned that I must control my prayers as I do not wish to bring death simply by my own powers. God is by my side, as you know.'

We all looked from her to Adam – she was convinced she could literally wish death upon someone, and he had bolstered the idea. I was beginning to wonder which of them was the barmier.

'Right, well, that's all clear then,' I remarked as some of the policemen exchanged glances. 'Peregrine's death was a simple matter in comparison to Sophia's. No complicated timings and very little preparation. The murderer had stolen his silver letter-opener ...' I held it up so that it caught the light. 'Things had a habit of disappearing around the house, so Peregrine wasn't unduly concerned. But then Sophia was murdered, and he began to fear for his own life – with good reason, as it turns out. His murder was straightforward. The dagger was probably tossed out as he watched, he leaned over the window sill to see where it landed, and he was pushed from behind – simple and effective. As far as I can discover, no one had an alibi for his time of death except Cooper, who had his own affairs to attend to.' I glanced at him. His colour had heightened, but he held himself with his usual stoicism. 'The only real clue was a smear of hair oil on the open window rail. It was in the exact spot that somebody leaning out to look below might touch with their hair. Peregrine didn't wear hair oil, did he, Adam?'

'No.' He shook his head.

'This was another feint, just as my pistol had been. Some time later we found a bottle which had been tossed out beyond the terrace.' I held up the shards in my jam jar, then placed it back on the table. 'It was designed to confuse matters, but it was the murderer's undoing. Something happened, something unanticipated. I can only imagine the murderer was about to be discovered by someone nearby and in a panic threw the bottle out of the window after Peregrine.'

I now straightened up and slowly turned to look each of them in the eyes. 'I am asking all of you to think about where you were that day and what you were doing, because one of you was the cause of the killer's panic. Who was it?'

Some of them returned my gaze but most retained stony expressions. Nobody volunteered any information. Uncle looked as though he were thoroughly enjoying the show – well, at least somebody was.

'Let us go back to the beginning, where this all started,' I went on, 'with the death of the fat man. In his pocket I found this piece of paper.' I picked it up from the evidence table – it had been one of the items I'd asked Swift to bring with him. He'd already requested files and evidence from my local constabulary as part of his earlier efforts to prove my guilt, and the paper had been amongst them.

'This is your writing, isn't it Natasha? It wasn't Sophia who sent George Pye to my home with an authentic bank draft to replace the fraudulent one, it was you. You realised that I could expose the whole charade and put everything in jeopardy. You had no idea how to find a bank draft, but you knew George Pye would, so you asked him to purchase it for you and sent him off to my house. George Pye was an ex-boxer, probably had some brain damage and couldn't remember the Countess's full title, so you wrote it down for him. And her name was vital because he was supposed to tell me that the new draft was from Sophia and that it had all been a terrible mistake. Isn't that right?'

'No, it is nonsense,' Natasha replied calmly. 'I often wrote such notes for her because she could not write English very well. She must have given it to him herself.'

I ignored her argument. 'Peregrine lent you the money, didn't he? He knew everything. The fraud, the truth about your husband, about who Sophia really was. And he would have continued controlling you just as Sophia had. So you killed him.

'A man killed him. You have merely devised this ridiculous story to hide your own guilt.'

'That's not true, 'Tasha,' Edgar said quietly.

We all turned to stare at him, as did his wife-to-be. 'Pardon?'

'You heard me. You lied about your whereabouts the day Peregrine died,' Edgar replied.

'How dare you!' Natasha turned to face him, the colour rising in her cheeks. 'How dare you implicate me in this. You will not speak against me, do you forget who I am?'

'I will never forget who you are, 'Tasha,' he replied. 'But you can't go round killing people – not in this country, you can't.'

Her face suddenly contorted and the rage erupted as she got to her feet, staring around in steel-eyed fury. 'You stupid little peasants. You provincial nonentities. You dare accuse me with your idiot laws? Laws are for little people – people like you, Edgar, with your paltry career, your dreary poverty and your tiny flat in that filthy city. If I had not been brought so low, I would never have stooped to the level of your insignificance. How dare you,' she screamed at him.

Edgar paled in the face of her ferocity but didn't flinch.

'I was courted by princes,' Natasha yelled. 'I was one of Russia's greatest heiresses, and I am reduced to this.' She raised a hand. 'This dull little house. It is nothingness. No grandeur. No majesty. I despise you all, you pathetic nobodies.' She looked like a cornered tiger – magnificent and terrifying. The policemen began to move in closer.

'You killed her, didn't you Natasha?' I accused her. 'You murdered Sophia. She wasn't just a liability, she was a blackmailer, and she had you under her thumb. Just as she sought to control us, so she controlled you. Your own servant became the puppet-master and she made you dance on her command.'

Natasha resumed her seat and brought herself back under control. She glared at us, her back rigid, her head slightly raised, the very embodiment of the high lady she had been bred to be.

'You guessed, didn't you, Edgar?' I asked, and all eyes swivelled in his direction.

Edgar glared at me taut with anger, then nodded slowly, reluctantly.

'When did you discover what she'd done?'

'The moment you asked where we'd been around the time Peregrine was killed. I was looking for 'Tasha, calling her name. Couldn't find Cooper and none of the servants answered my bell, so I went looking for her. She must have heard me and thrown the bottle out of the window before coming downstairs.'

'The bottle was yours, I assume?'

'Yes.' He nodded. 'I realised it was gone, but until now I had no idea where it was.'

'She implicated you to divert attention from herself.'

'I do realise that, Lennox,' he snapped.

'You must have suspected before today, Edgar. In fact, I know you did.' Our conversation from yesterday was still fresh in my mind.

'Yes, but I rather think you've opened my eyes wider with your theatricals.'

'Natasha?' I said to her.

Inspector Swift had now stepped forward.

'Madam. Please stand up and hold out your hands,' he ordered. He slipped a pair of handcuffs from his pocket, when suddenly she turned the velvet bag and clutched it tightly. A shot rang out.

We froze, horrified, and stared at her. She'd hidden a gun in the velvet bag and hadn't even withdrawn it to pull the trigger. The bullet had hit her in the chest. Blood began to well out and spread across the dusky-rose fabric of her dress as she lay slumped in her chair, eyes staring vacantly at the ceiling.

The rest was mayhem. Uncle toppled over in horror. Cooper grabbed him and practically dragged him from the room. Edgar cried out and tried to revive Natasha and we had to pull him off. Gertrude stared fascinated at the body, then turned to my table of evidence, eyeing the necklace, and I had to yell at Adam to take his wife back to their suite. The police started shouting; one of them drew his whistle and blew it until Swift snapped at him to shut up. Hearing the commotion, various servants came running. Cooper ordered them back to work as he tried to get Uncle to his rooms. I'd had enough and helped myself to a brandy, then sat next to the fire until some sort of order was restored and Swift eventually made us leave the room while a doctor was called, although it was a bit late: Natasha Czerina Orlakov-Palen was as dead as any one of her victims.

CHAPTER 21

The rest of the day passed strangely. Police came and went, then a doctor followed by an ambulance arrived and poor Natasha was stretchered away. Peregrine was retrieved from his nest in the straw and he too was carted off. Statements were taken, we were repeatedly questioned and our details written and rewritten, then rooms were searched and dusted with quantities of powder.

After I'd made another statement to Swift in the smoking room, which brought on a peculiar feeling of déjà-vu, I was released and retreated to my rooms with my dog, where I stoked up the fire and read *Moby Dick* as an antidote to the frenzy the day had rained upon us.

I couldn't really concentrate on my book; I wanted to find Edgar and commiserate with him, try to talk things through – but the police decided he could be an accessory to the murders and gave him the third degree, before warning him that he was under house arrest and was not to leave the premises until further notice.

It was very late in the evening when we were finally

free of them all, and I made my way to Uncle's rooms to find Edgar already there and Uncle pouring liquor into him by way of a remedy to his woes.

'Dark day,' Uncle said to me by way of greeting.

'Yes,' I agreed, running my hand through my hair.

Cooper was there as well, and handed me a glass of the best brandy. I think he'd had a tough time of it, too. 'Where are the Kingsleys?' I asked him.

'In their suite, sir, preparing to leave tomorrow.'

'Thank God for that. Make sure Miss Gertrude doesn't snaffle anything important.'

'Certainly, sir – and it is Lady Gertrude now: Sir Peregrine's title has passed to his son and heir.'

'Sir Adam bloody Kingsley? He'll be preening himself on that one,' I replied in exasperation.

'Lennox,' Edgar said to me. 'Bloody awful, wasn't it?'

I let a long sigh escape me as I settled by the fire with them and took a warming sip of my drink. 'It was. And I am so very sorry about the outcome, Edgar.'

'My own fault,' he said. He looked miserable: tie askew, smart suit rumpled, hair in desperate need of a comb and oil. 'So much for my good judgement; if this gets out I can wave goodbye to my career.'

'You did surprise me, Heathcliff,' Uncle said. 'Never thought you'd actually achieve anything at all but look at you – two murders solved and you've saved Edgar from marrying a vixen. She'd have probably murdered me one day. And you! It was a near miss for us all.'

'Uncle!' Edgar retorted sharply. 'Sophia may not have

been a killer but she was certainly Machiavellian; she'd have had us all on strings if you'd married her.'

Uncle gave a quiet chuckle. 'Yes, but it would have been so stimulating, crossing swords with the lady. What a ride it would have been.'

Edgar and I looked at him and shook our heads; we'd both be careful to keep him well away from the ladies from now on.

'May I ask a question, sir?' Cooper turned to me.

'Of course, fire away.'

'The wax, sir – there was talk of wax, and I'd heard from the outside staff that you had been enquiring of Mr Biggs the butcher about it, sir.'

'Yes,' Uncle added. 'What was all this talk of delayed bangs?'

I'd had to explain to Inspector Swift those very same details this morning, so the story came readily to the tongue and I quickly told them how it all went.

'But there was no smell of burned feathers, and I think I'd have noticed it the night Sophia died,' Edgar commented.

'Yes, the wax wasn't from the butchery, it was from Natasha's bathroom,' I replied.

'What the hell were you doing in there?' Edgar snapped.

'Looking for wax, of course! I found it last night while you were all at dinner.'

'What do ladies use wax for?' Uncle asked.

'Hair removal,' I replied, 'on their legs, you know. Stockings.'

'Ah, yes, how very clever of you, my boy,' Uncle remarked, and drifted off into a reverie – probably concerning his late fiancée and stockings.

Cooper became embarrassed at such talk and excused himself.

I turned to Edgar. 'What are you going to do now, old boy? Can't leave things as they are.'

He stared into the flames and didn't answer. I topped up his glass by way of encouragement.

'I wish I knew,' he said at last. 'I'm out from under the debt I owed Sophia but there's plenty more I have to cover. And I think matrimony as a way out has rather lost its appeal.'

'Ha,' I laughed quietly. 'May I make a suggestion?'

'Yes, of course.'

'Make this house your base for a while; rent out Eaton Square. It'll lighten your load, might even put some money in your pocket. And with Peregrine's tentacles finally removed, you could take over, put things on a good footing here and take the income he was paid. Might just save the place.'

Edgar looked at me in surprise. 'I'll consider it,' he replied thoughtfully. 'It would fit in with my career ... I could come down here between postings,' he mused.

'I would like that very much, Edgar,' Uncle said.

Edgar looked at me. 'What do you intend to do?'

'Celebrate the New Year with you then I'm going home with my dog,' I told him.

'Talking of your home, Lennox. The fat man?' Edgar

asked. 'What did you say happened to his hat and the bank draft?'

'The man who drove the car must have stolen it,' I replied. 'Thought I'd told you?'

'Possibly,' he frowned. 'If he hadn't died that day this could have turned out very differently. It seems so very bizarre that he should die on your doorstep.'

'Ah, well, I have a confession to make,' I replied. They both turned to stare at me. 'His heart attack was probably caused by being forced to run, an activity for which he was patently ill-equipped.'

'Lennox. You didn't force the man to run, did you?' Uncle demanded.

'No, Fogg chased him. He may be a useless gun dog, but he'll certainly chase delivery boys, or postmen, or in this case a messenger. The fat man walked down the drive from the gateway, and Fogg barked. The man ran, and Fogg ran after him. There were snags in the man's trousers where Fogg had bitten into them – it was very obvious what had happened.'

The guilty party was snoring at our feet on the hearthrug, oblivious to it all. We looked down at him.

'So the dog did it,' Uncle remarked, and we all laughed

I do hope you enjoyed this book. If you would like to keep up to date with this series, you can do so on the Karen Menuhin readers page here…

https://karenmenuhin.com/

By signing up you will be updated about latest releases, stories, pics and news, including Mr Fogg, Tubbs and more. It would be great to see you there!

***

Murder at Melrose Court is the first book in the Heathcliff Lennox series.

The Black Cat Murders is the second book.

The Curse of Braeburn Castle is the third book.

Death in Damascus is the fourth book.

The Monks Hood Murders is the fifth book.

If you like this book, please leave a nice review!! It really helps.

If you feel there is something amiss, please do get in touch with me at karen@littledogpublishing.com and I'll do all I can to help.

A little about Karen Baugh Menuhin

1920s, Cozy crime, Traditional Detectives, Downton Abbey – I love them!

Along with my family, my dog and my cat.

At 60 I decided to write, I don't know why but suddenly the stories came pouring out, along with the characters. Eccentric Uncles, stalwart butlers, idiosyncratic servants, machinating Countesses, and the hapless Major Heathcliff Lennox.

A whole world built itself upon the page and I just followed along...

An itinerate traveller all my life. I grew up in the military, often on RAF bases but preferring to be in the countryside when we could. I adore whodunnits.

I have two amazing sons – Jonathan and Sam Baugh and their wives, Laura and Wendy, and five grandchildren, Charlie, Joshua, Isabella-Rose, Scarlett and Hugo.

I am married to Krov, my wonderful husband, who is a retired film maker and eldest son of the violinist, Yehudi Menuhin. We live in the Cotswolds.

For more information my address is:
karen@littledogpublishing.com

Made in the USA
Middletown, DE
15 December 2020